SEAWEED

Anthony E. Miller

Whimsical Publications, LLC

Florida

To purchase the authorized electronic edition of *Seaweed*, visit
www.whimsicalpublications.com

Cover art by Traci Markou
Editing by Melissa Hosack

ISBN-13: 978-1-940707-78-5

Published by
Whimsical Publications, LLC
Florida

One day, he was helping her with the EU paperwork and they happened to get onto what the land the nuns owned was actually worth.

"What do you mean what's it worth?" asked Mr. Simbold.

"Well, the whole thing, I suppose. The farm, the house, the guesthouse, the chapel...the whole place," replied Sister Quiteria.

"Isn't that a bit of an earthly question?" teased Mr. Simbold.

"Well, it's a practical question," said Sister Quiteria. "You know we may have to sell or move some time."

"Really?" said Mr. Simbold. "Surely not in the immediate future?"

"Well, it's no secret," said Sister Quiteria, "that we sometimes have a lot of difficulty breaking even and that we rely in no small part on the sale of Mother Rosalinda's art."

"But surely that's very cynical? Not very Godly?"

"I know what you're saying, Mr. Simbold," she said, "but it's up to God when he takes each of us and I'm sure God would want us to plan for the future. If he literally told us what to do all the time. there'd be no part for us to play, would there?"

"I suppose not."

"Of course the Mother House would help us out if it turned out we hit a sudden financial shortfall—that is after all how we moved here in the first place...but nevertheless, we do have to think if staying here is the best way to pursue our mission."

"I think it is," said Mr. Simbold.

"That's because it's convenient for you," said Sister Quiteria. Mr. Simbold thought this slightly rude. She continued. "I don't mean that in a nasty way. We all seek out what is easy. It is a beautiful and historical place here, but you must remember we didn't go into a Convent in order to own things, including the buildings themselves."

Mr. Simbold gave her a look as if to say, "*Are you having me on?*"

Sister Quiteria gave Mr. Simbold a look as if to say, "*Don't be stupid. I'm a nun.*"

"All I'm asking is...could you make some enquiries?"

"Some enquiries?"

"About potentially selling the building and grounds and what it would be worth on the open market. I know it may seem an odd request, but Mother Rosalinda would be very grateful. The thing is, you see, we don't want to start a rumour in the village or in the press...so things need to be tackled with some tact and diplomacy."

"And you think I have those qualities?" said Mr. Simbold.

"Well, you are a politician. Aren't you supposed to have them?" said Sister Quiteria. "And you are a solicitor, so technically you'd know the paperwork if and when we decide to sell."

"Well, you can sell without a solicitor these days," said Mr. Simbold. "What you can't do is sell without publicity. The moment you go to an estate agent, people will know it's on the market."

Sister Quiteria smiled. "We may not be planning to sell the place to just any bidder. We may already have another buyer in mind...another religious community. With more members. The question then is knowing a fair price. In which case we'd need someone to give us a fair valuation and to arrange exchange of contracts. In my experience, a lot of things that seem complicated can be made much simpler...so long as you have the right kind of help. Can't they?"

"I suppose so," said Mr. Simbold.

"Just keep it under your hat a bit. And we'll keep things..."

"Beneath your veils?"

"Exactly. Now then, tea?"

Just then Father Baines ran into the room without knocking. Mr. Simbold was pissed off. Baines had only just gone back out in the fields instead of hanging round the shop skiving and moaning how he was better than the manure that covered his boots. Mr. Simbold was about to remonstrate with him for not knocking when he looked at him again. He was muddy top to bottom—he had obviously fallen over. There was blood down his arm...but his coat was not torn. It was not his blood. He was whiter than expected, even in the cutting wind outside.

"Come quick!" he shouted. "And call an ambulance."

Chapter One

There are moments in time that are wrong. Sister Quiteria's vows were one of them. Superficially, this was due to Father Baines.

Father Baines was an unpleasant bore. Let's face it, religion was fairly boring—or at least not exciting—but Father Baines could take that boredom or lack of excitement to a different and quite unpleasant level. What made this moment particularly unpleasant to Sister Quiteria was that he seemed to take it upon himself to make an event that was supposed to be about her—her fully joining with the community and with Jesus—about him and secular society's modern evils. Not that secular society didn't have modern evils, but was now the time to explore them? It wasn't laid on with a trowel, but it was there—his opinions. They got into everything.

Of course Father Baines would have said that they were God's opinions. However, it seemed to Sister Quiteria that if they were God's opinions, God wasn't quite as forthright at expressing them as Father Baines. Father Baines had a way of saying things that seemed to be not saying things, but was actually worse than being outwardly critical. It was so absolutely ridiculous too. What could be a better example of preaching to the converted, after all, than forcing your views on the wickedness of secular word on nuns? Frankly, none of them cared about the secular world. It was the outside. Their primary relationship thought Sister Quiteria was with God—not the media or the laity. Maybe it wouldn't have been so bad if Sister Quiteria had had relatives there to distract her, but they couldn't come...so she didn't. Most of them were dead.

Actually, Sister Quiteria wasn't that religious. She just went along with it all for her own reasons. She liked being there. She liked being away from people. She liked the soli-tude—or as near to solitude as she could get—after years of having a job where interacting with other people had been, to put it mildly, a bit of an interpersonal risk. As to religion, well, there might be something in it. Not completely believing in the afterlife seemed a silly reason to her not to be a nun. After all, there were plenty of people in other careers who had no real belief or interest in what they did. They just faked it. That was not to say she didn't enjoy having an im-aginary conversation with Jesus from time to time, but that didn't mean she actually believed he was there. She believed he'd existed, but beyond that...well, she had to use her im-agination a bit. Sister Quiteria was a brutal realist, but she still had a vivid imagination.

Sister Quiteria liked institutions and order, and their insti-tutionalised life was highly ordered. Where it wasn't ordered, she was quite good at making suggestions to make it more ordered and more efficient. As she explained to Mother Rosalinda, "Just because we're not out to make money doesn't mean we can't run efficiently. The more businesslike we are, the more time there should be left over for us to pray in." This wasn't a wildly popular opinion in the convent, but she stuck to it, and her success in implementing it had created equal volumes of quiet admiration and passive-aggressive resentment on behalf of the other sisters.

It was a mystery to Sister Quiteria why they had got stuck with Father Baines. She knew there was a shortage of priests, but there must be others. Why were they stuck with a man who seemed to spend most of his time having online rows with the gay community and the BHA, and had been Stonewall's bigot of the year in the past and seemed so per-petually angry about it? Not that she knew all the ins and outs. Some of the rumours of his bust-ups may have been greatly exaggerated, but she guessed the essence of what the other nuns said behind his back was true. Indeed, it probably was all true, but Sister Quiteria wasn't going to Google it. After all, his opinions didn't bother her in terms of the nature of the opinions themselves, but it still bothered her that Father Baines was so not-at-peace with himself in such a peaceful place. It was annoying.

Even when he wasn't crowbarring his opinions into everything, she could sense his anger there somewhere under the surface. One might call it a chip on the shoulder if it was the result of some kind of injustice, but Sister Quiteria was unaware of any real injustices being visited on Father Baines apart from the time some youths stole his bicycle, which was about the most exciting thing that had happened in the village in the last decade.

The nuns, of course, didn't use the Internet...much...but there was a telephone and a phone box just round the corner if they wanted to make a phone call and have it not appear on the phone bill. Sister Quiteria was sure she wasn't the only one with a smartphone.

Anyway, it was her day, so she felt within her rights to mentally shut Father Baines out and occasionally imagine him being waterboarded or gently tortured. Otherwise, it had been a lovely day so far. The singing was good and relatively in tune for a change. There were always a few nuns out of tune, but so what? It wasn't *X Factor*. The light made nice coloured patterns on the carpet as it streamed through the stained glass windows. Then just as Father Baines was embarking on a particularly painful section on white martyrdom, there was a piercing scream.

Mother Rosalinda had collapsed. Sister Maria picked her up and helped her back into her choir stall. Sister Quiteria hurried to help too. The other two nearest nuns would have helped as well, but both were over eighty and frankly something of a financial burden to carry for the other nuns at the best of times. This was particularly evident where the physical aspects of their working lives were concerned—like picking things and people up.

Sister Margaret was dispatched to use the telephone to call Doctor Fay Bones as Sister Margaret was generally allowed to use the telephone...along with Mother Rosalinda who obviously couldn't use the telephone at the moment as she was unconscious. Of course, no one ever said explicitly, "You cannot use the telephone." But they all knew what the rule was and observed it. If they didn't, what would be the point in being there? It wasn't as if Mother Rosalinda was checking the bill. Sister Margaret might do so if she was bored, but probably not.

Mother Rosalinda was taken back to her cell. Doctor Fay

Bones arrived. Mother Rosalinda recovered consciousness quickly, but seemed to be in some pain. An ambulance was called eventually. They probably should have called an ambulance in the first place, but then it was seldom they needed outside help, so maybe it seemed strange to call 999 immediately. An overreaction? None of them were that ill usually. An advantage of a fairly enclosed community did seem to be a lack of cold and flu.

— ❦ —

Sister Quiteria and Sister Margaret got back with Mother Rosalinda from the hospital at 11 a.m. the following morning. Mother Rosalinda wanted to get back to work straight away, but Sister Margaret insisted she rest for the day in her cell. Mother Rosalinda tried to...despite the fact that Sister Margaret had forgotten to switch off the propane powered gas gun in the adjacent field. Mother Rosalinda didn't ask her to because she worried too much about the birds eating their crops, so she just lay quietly, slightly drifting off in a bored way then being woken up again and sometimes saying a prayer in between each random *BANG!...BANG!...BANG!...BANG!...BANG!* Still, eventually, she nodded off into the lower stages of non-rapid eye movement sleep if not deep sleep.

Oh well, thought Sister Quiteria, at least she had taken her vows even if the service hadn't ended as they'd expected, and at least they'd been saved more of Father Baines' boring sermon.

— ❦ —

Later, Mother Rosalinda and some of the other nuns commiserated with Sister Quiteria about how awful it must be to have her acceptance into the community turned into such a memorable-for-the-wrong-reasons event. Sister Quiteria went through the motions of looking dismayed, but fortunately, the drama of Mother Rosalinda's collapse quickly put such concerns into the shade as immediate fears took over from what seemed selfish commiserations.

"It's usually such a joyous occasion," said Mother Rosalinda.

"Yes, but it is not that important how I feel, Mother Rosalinda. It is far more important we find out what is wrong with you," said Sister Quiteria.

"That is very kind of you, Sister Quiteria," said Mother Rosalinda. "It may all seem incomprehensible to us, but...all these things must happen for a reason, mustn't they?"

"They must," said Sister Quiteria.

Chapter Two

Doctor Fay Bones was vague. Everyone said so. About everything he did. He was desperately shy of people, which always made his patients feel even more uncomfortable and afraid than they needed to be. This made the fact that he didn't find it easy to find out what was wrong with Mother Rosalinda more frightening for her. Mostly, he sent her for tests—lots of them. Eventually, she went to a consultant. Only then did it start to become faintly less opaque.

Sister Margaret and Sister Quiteria took turns driving Mother Rosalinda to all these appointments in "the car." Sister Quiteria had christened the car "the car." It was a vomit yellow Austin Allegro nearing 100,000 miles on the clock that supplied all the nuns' very occasional motoring needs. It was a miserable experience to drive, which added to the miserable experience of waiting in waiting rooms. These experiences weren't made less miserable by the fact that Sister Quiteria hardly drove at all these days except the tractor and could only barely remember how to do it. It made going there even more frightening than it needed to be.

Still, they deluded themselves that this ancient machine was somehow less silly than simply calling a taxi. Perhaps it was a sort of subconscious self-punishment or penance for going outside the walls of the convent—a deterrent. They could go outside the grounds, but it would have to be in that thing. Most of the convent was surrounded by a large stone wall. This was because it had originally been a Monastery before Henry VIII closed them all and had only been reopened as a convent in the early 20th century. Both the wall and the car were depressing. One because it was visually ominous. The other because it was visually revolting.

Doctor Fay Bones was a nervous, fidgety man and Mother Rosalinda was not the most demanding of NHS "customers," but even she eventually started to tire of the inability of either her GP or the medical fraternity to supply a clear explanation of why she'd fallen over.

"I don't think it was a stroke," said Doctor Fay Bones. "Sometimes people collapse and we really don't know why. It can be a bit of a mystery." This was one of his most particularly unhelpful comments. Sister Quiteria and Mother Rosalinda looked at each other so much as to say, "*Mystery is our business. We could have stayed at home if we needed more of that.*" More mystery there was, though, and more tests until an x-ray, CT scan, and guided needle biopsy revealed that Mother Rosalinda had the early stages of small cell lung cancer.

There were many more appointments, and the NHS being the NHS, some of them were cancelled and rescheduled incorrectly, meaning that instead of being able to do her quota of farm work, Mother Rosalinda lost even more time to sitting in waiting rooms. This theoretically freed up more time for prayer, but somehow it was hard to pray in waiting rooms. At the very least it was neither ideal nor productive. Mother Rosalinda felt more guilt when she started to realise she was mostly praying about herself and not other people. Eventually, at their weekly planning meeting, she raised the obvious question. "Should I step down as Mother Superior?"

"No, no," they answered collectively.

"I'm not feeling too unwell, you understand." They all knew she understated the problem. "But obviously when the chemotherapy starts, I won't be able to do as much...certainly not as much physically as I can now...and I'm not sure I'll be able to concentrate on things as much. I mean, my concentration may go. I also have paintings to finish for the exhibition coming up..."

They all pondered the problem quietly while trying to keep a veneer of serenity. Sister Quiteria pondered most. She always resented—and she was certain some of the others secretly resented—Mother Rosalinda's painting. Mother Rosalinda had always painted and, since she had become a nun, her painting had taken on more religious themes, but it just seemed somehow not quite right for her to have an individual career in the fine arts while the rest of them spent their time dealing with manure and silage...and ploughing the seed and scattering...and in the day to day running of a medium-sized arable farm...and dealing with the various whims and caprices of the guests in the guesthouse when not praying and...

Mother Rosalinda had this other life. This strange alien life which seemed on the surface to be compatible with the rule of Saint Benedict...but was it? The thing was, it seemed in some way to confer on her a kind of celebrity. A very low kind of celebrity. A very remote kind. Still a celebrity nonetheless. Sometimes, she would be asked to go to a gallery opening. Occasionally, she would appear on television...and although the rest of them didn't have a television, they felt it a bit strange. Mother Rosalinda had studied at the Royal Academy of Arts. She had exhibited at the Tate. She had had a successful career as a painter before joining. Surely God wouldn't want her to stop painting, would he? If nothing else, it brought in the convent a fair bit of money. Still, it seemed wrong to Sister Quiteria...or at least bending the rules somehow. However, it might not have been.

"We can always come up with a new rota?" said Sister Margaret. A new rota was Sister Margaret's solution to almost everything. "I mean, really you're not just our practical but our spiritual leader, Mother Rosalinda, and do we want to rush to change that if we don't need to?"

"Crawler," thought Sister Quiteria. It was clear to her that Sister Margaret had desires to run the community.

"I agree," said Sister Maria. Others agreed too. Agreement was something nuns were good at. At least superficial agreements.

"I think we should think about it carefully," said Sister Quiteria. "I mean all of it. We are using some heavy machinery. We don't want there to be accidents because someone is over-tired. We're going to need to review the rota...quite a bit...aren't we?"

There was an awkward silence.

"I agree it is a difficult situation," said Mother Rosalinda, "but we must put our faith in Jesus. Remember what he tells us in Luke 12, 'do not worry about your life, what you will eat, or about your body, what you will wear. For life is more than food, and the body more than clothing.'"

"Consider the ravens: they neither sow nor reap, they have neither storehouse nor barn, and yet God feeds them," enjoined Sister Margaret.

"Of how much more value are you than the birds!" added Sister Maria.

"Yes, I know," said Sister Quiteria, "but all the same...I'm sure Jesus didn't mean for us to have no plans at all. We should all give it some thought."

"Perhaps we can get some temporary help from outside?" said Sister Margaret.

"Aren't we supposed to be self-sufficient...sort of?" said Sister Quiteria, fearing that outside help was more likely to mean seeing more of Father Baines than the materialisation of a home help...or something actually practical.

"We are meant to be dedicating our lives individually and collectively to Jesus," said Mother Rosalinda. "The best way to do that is something I shall have to pray about."

Sister Quiteria would like to have believed that prayer would provide a radical solution to these problems, but somehow she knew the reality would most likely be they would be seeing a lot more of Father Baines. She sometimes wondered if Baines and Mother Rosalinda fancied each other...but, of course, that was silly. Mother Rosalinda was married to Jesus.

Chapter Three

Mother Rosalinda's first solution to the logistical problems was a new rota. Mother Rosalinda's solution to most logistical problems was usually a new rota. Actually, it was Sister Margaret's solution, but as Mother Rosalinda implemented it, she saw it as her solution first.

The nuns had lots of rotas. Indeed sometimes Sister Quiteria thought that the only people with more rotas than their order were Agusta and Westland the helicopter manufacturers. To be fair to Mother Rosalinda and Sister Margaret, they were pretty good at rotas, but they could, Sister Quiteria often thought, be better if they had more management experience. Sister Margaret had previously been a head teacher in the private sector before joining the order, but it wasn't the same as a proper managerial role, Sister Quiteria often thought. She had suggested they go on a management course once, but it had not gone down very well. They tried to run the farm, the guesthouse, the shop, and the other businesses as efficiently as they could, but as soon as Sister Quiteria said words like "critical chain project management," some nun would take it as a challenge to some other nun's authority.

One of the delusions people had about monastic life was that there wasn't a lot to do. On the contrary, since the primary object of monastic life was prayer, this actually created less time to do everything else. Everything else then had to be fitted around this. If someone were to draw a cost-quality-time triangle, the one thing the nuns would be shown to be most short of would be time. There was ploughing, dealing with the silage and manure, looking after the bird scarers, looking after the small guest house, arranging the coming ecumenical conference, and giving religious instruction to local schoolchildren. All of this had to be fitted into less and less time to create more and more time for prayer. Add to this that different nuns were better at some tasks than others and there were chores such as spreading the seaweed on the fields that everyone tried to get out of...and they had a recipe for internal political conflict that would make the Labour Party under Michael Foot seem a model of social unity.

For the nuns, seaweed was actually quite a popular and, more importantly, cheap fertiliser. It was rich in nitrogen, as could be deduced from the speed with which it repelled tourists away from the beaches if left there too long. Consequently, the local Council, which liked to see tourists taking leisurely strolls along the front rather than running a mile, did various deals with anybody who would remove it cheaply. Sister Margaret had signed a contract with them to remove some of their seaweed and spread it on the nuns' fields. She imagined this to be to their mutual advantage.

Unfortunately, seaweed was somewhat high in salt, so they had to leave it in a huge pile for a while before spreading it in the hope that the rain would wash some of the salt away—otherwise they were in danger of killing their worms. Neither could they desalinate it quickly by throwing water over it as this risked washing away the alginates in it that were supposedly valuable. The result was that if the wind was in the wrong direction for long periods of time, the entire convent smelled like an open sewer. The longer they had to leave the seaweed before spreading it, the more pungent its aroma seemed to become, with the result that there were few volunteers for the task of spreading it. As a result of this and other equally unpleasant tasks about the farm, the rotas became very important and argued over very hotly but politely.

Eventually, finding that the decrease in womanpower was starting to mean the seaweed was indeed being spread less often, Mother Rosalinda resolved to do something. Her enthusiasm to make things more efficient in this area may have had something to do with the fact that her painting "studio" was near to a large pile of seaweed and was smelling more and more putrid as a result. There were a limited number of options as to what she could do, but feeling that dealing with the antipathy between Father Baines and some of the other nuns was only a slightly lesser evil than the putrid smell, she rang Father Baines and asked if he knew of anyone else who could lend a hand...which was her way of asking him to lend a hand.

"This can't go on," she said. "The guests in the guest-house may stop paying to stay here if they continue having to breathe more nitrous compounds than a drain inspector." Actually, the smell wasn't that bad near the guesthouse, but to Mother Rosalinda, that wasn't the point.

Father Baines said he'd have to ask his bishop, who was very busy, and he suspected the answer may be "no" because he had lots of masses to say.

However, it just so happened that Bishop O'Flarty was visiting that week for the yearly blessing of the relics of St. Ethelbert (the nuns had an unidentified piece of dry skin in an elaborate pewter box) and Bishop O'Flarty thought it was a great idea.

—⚬⚭⚬—

"You're not that busy. They need help. You can help them," Bishop O'Flarty told Father Baines on the phone.

"I am busy, John. I've got two parishes to run."

"I banned you from writing on the Internet, which seemed to be taking up most of your time," said the bishop. "So you should have lots more time than you used to."

"I thought you said that was a period of reflection. Not a ban," said Father Baines.

"I did," said Bishop O'Flarty. "And I think you'd reflect better on authority within the church by helping Mother Rosalinda to shift some of her seaweed manure."

"Well, I don't think that's what I'm here for..."

"Well, it is. Besides which," replied the bishop, thinking that perhaps he should try a different, more tactful approach, "you are the one whose vocation seems so concerned with dissent in the church. If that is your vocation, you might find a way of exercising it there by keeping me a bit more informed of what goes on. It will only be temporary while Mother Rosalinda is undergoing treatment for her cancer. Tending the sick is an act of Christian charity. And so is spreading the sick's manure."

"What do you mean?" asked Father Baines. "Why can't their Mother House send them someone to help?"

"Their Mother House has already sent them someone. Sister Maria," said the bishop, "who, as you probably don't know because you spend all your time scouring the papers looking for dirt on your fellow English clergy rather than those in Italy, has been having a little difficulty recently with the Congregation for the Doctrine of the faith..."

"Oh."

"Exactly. She seems to have become enamoured of a rather unsavoury brand of radical feminism...so I'd like it if you can to keep an eye on things."

"Yes."

—⁓⊙⊙⁓—

The following Monday, Father Baines found himself spreading toxic smelling seaweed over a field that would hold cauliflowers rather than spreading his toxic opinions on internal church heretics over the Internet using a pseudonym. He was not pleased. Neither was Sister Quiteria, who hated him. Sister Maria, who knew of his reputation, was actually not that bothered by it as it gave her somebody to upset regularly. They actually had quite interesting rows while throwing around the seaweed, and began to bond a bit despite the toxic smell and what they both regarded as the other's equally toxic opinions.

Soon Sister Margaret found herself drawing up yet another new over-complicated rota on the orders of Mother Rosalinda that Mother Rosalinda seemed to take the credit for. Mother Rosalinda continued to be pleased with herself for having the great idea of involving Father Baines and while the nuns felt uneasy about him being there, no one felt up to contradicting Mother Rosalinda. Firstly, because she was ill, and secondly, because they liked avoiding the seaweed...so for a while no one said anything. Not even Sister Quiteria.

Chapter Four

Sister Margaret's new rota had the disadvantage that Sister Quiteria now seemed to be spending a lot more time in the shop, and Sister Maria was spending more time spreading seaweed manure. This should not have been a disadvantage to Sister Quiteria, but it was.

At some point, it had been thought that it might be a good idea to have a larger shop to sell their farm produce, perfumes (why they had to make perfume, Sister Quiteria didn't know) and Mother Rosalinda's paintings. Mother Rosalinda had the idea of turning it into part museum as well, despite them knowing nothing about how to run a museum. This idea never actually went anywhere much, but nevertheless, Father Baines had found some old gas masks and garden implements with which to help give the impression they'd been there forever rather than just reoccupying the old derelict buildings in 1937 for fear that Mussolini might eventually make things too difficult for the order in Italy. So the "shop" was something of a hotchpotch of muddled aims...and much like many of the other endeavours the nuns engaged in, it might have been done better with more help from outside. Some of the other nuns thought staffing the shop was a bit of a cushy number, but Sister Quiteria, who actually worked there, was not happy there. She'd rather have been outdoors. Even if it meant being with seaweed.

For a start, not that many people wanted to buy much from the shop in person and so she spent a lot of time parcelling things up for mail order. Despite the smells and the bitter wind from the North Sea that cut away any body heat they could trap under a habit or coat, the outside was at least a little less dull than the inside. Also, paradoxically, the inside seemed to be colder than the outside. The heating wasn't on all the time and she could hear the wind, which made her feel cold even if she was not. Being still a lot made Sister Quiteria feel colder, and pacing the room didn't heat her up. She'd rather be out in the open. At least she knew how the machinery worked.

Despite having been at the Convent most of her adult life, Sister Margaret still didn't seem to know her PTO shaft from her elbow. "How do you fix the guard again?" she would moan, and Sister Quiteria would have to leave what she was doing and show her for the 96th time. Then come back again from out of the cold to sit in the cold.

Sister Quiteria was of the general opinion that the nuns were shit at farming. The prices of their produce were relatively competitive as far as Supermarket sales went—even ASDA had some qualms about ripping off nuns. However, locally they were being undercut by a farm shop not a mile down the road. That farm's militant atheist proprietor, Mr. Ward, took great delight in expending an ever increasing volume of money on advertising boards crassly stating that there was "nun cheaper" than his food round here. Unfortunately, this was literally true and on the whole it was down to economies of scale.

Without the tax advantages that came from being a religious community, it was doubtful the nuns would have been able to compete commercially at all. The boundaries of their land had been defined in the 11th century with reference to how far one of the nuns' oxen had roamed, and this had left the farm a shape that was not ideal for modern machinery. Added to that, the land was crossed by many rights of way, which they were supposed to plough around not over.

However, as ploughing round them was impractical, they'd have to plough over them, upsetting the villagers who resented the disappearances of the shortcuts and made their annoyance known by walking over the fields where they imagined the paths had been. Where they imagined the paths had been was not usually where they actually were, and the result was that the crops got damaged. Still, lots of people visiting from the town used to treat the fields as their own private garden anyway, oblivious to the fact it was working land, so what did it matter? Sister Quiteria often used to fantasise about shooting them. Unfortunately, such an action would have been deemed un-Christian. Perhaps this was the reason she was working indoors while Sister Maria had managed to negotiate spending more time in the field by sucking up to Sister Margaret...well, that and the fact they both spoke Italian. Then again, Sister Quiteria had told them in her previous lay life she had worked for an accountancy firm, so maybe she'd been the architect of her own misfortune here. Still, she could hardly claim to have been a painter. She had to tell them something.

On top of dealing with angry correspondents on eBay and Amazon who didn't understand why their orders of perfumes, cosmetics, jams, and farm produce were delayed to fit into a life of prayer, Sister Quiteria seemed to have to do the bulk of the accounts as well. She also had to fit that around dealing with any capricious requests from the guests in the guest house. The guest house had also seemed a simple idea at the time, but for some reason, many of the people who decided to stay there because they'd discovered the rooms were cheaper than the local hotels still imagined they could expect hotel service from nuns.

Bending the rules of the order slightly, Sister Quiteria made an effort to get to know them all and all their business. There were those who came on religious retreats, those who wanted somewhere to stay overnight when working locally, those affiliated to the RCC's various satellite lay orders like the Knights of St. Columba for lad culture, the St. Vincent de Paul Society for boring other people into Catholicism and Opus Dei...the wannabe monastics...and then there were people who used the rooms for reasons one could only ponder on.

Most strange amongst these was their local MEP Mr. Simon Simbold. Mr. Simbold had started hiring rooms as a place from which to conduct his constituency surgeries. As time went on, however, he started hiring a room as somewhere to stay overnight as his secretary Ms. Thrusk lived in the village. This caused much local gossip. The excuse he mobilised for this was that he had a large constituency and had to commute between there and Europe, and the convent was conveniently located for the Eurostar terminal. If anyone believed that, thought Sister Quiteria, they must be really thick. Fortunately, a lot of the nuns were really thick and even the ones that weren't were not allowed out, and as they weren't allowed out, there was little chance of gossip spreading...except amongst the nuns themselves who generally turned a blind eye to whatever it was that was going on, because it was none of their business and they needed the money. "Judge not lest you lose a customer," Mother Rosalinda used to say to her. It was clear to both of them that Mr. Simbold was having an affair. They thought they should do something, but they didn't...apart from trying to get him to go to confession and scowling at him when he received "the sacrament".

All this was in the middle rather than the back of Sister Quiteria's mind when Mr. Simbold came into the shop one day in search of supplies—chiefly alcohol, teabags, and newspapers, all of which he consumed in industrial quantities. Sister Quiteria, having had a relatively quiet time that morning, had been wading through the accounts to kill two birds with one stone...an exercise in efficiency which she knew would not be appreciated.

"Busy?" asked Mr. Simbold.

"Always seem to be," said Sister Quiteria. "It's the accounts that do me in."

"Surely they can't be that complicated," said Simbold. "Aren't you exempt from a whole load of taxes and that?"

"Well, yes," said Quiteria. "But we still have to keep an eye on incomings and outgoings."

"Why? Don't you trust each other?" joked Mr. Simbold. He liked joking with them, but always felt his jokes fell flat...which indeed this one did.

Sister Quiteria saw her opportunity. "You wouldn't lend me a hand some time, would you?"

Mr. Simbold did a double-take. His double chin vibrated, and he ejected a small but audible fart, which he pretended not to have heard. Continuing the conversation as if nothing had happened, he asked, "Am I allowed?"

"Well, I wouldn't ask if it wasn't your background and you weren't here so often."

"Is there a problem," asked Mr. Simbold, "with me being here so often?"

"No, not at all. We like having you," said Sister Quiteria, "and I'm sure the gay rights activists won't dump any more manure outside the front gate again now the police have told them not to."

"I think that very much depends on what our more ob-tuse members decide to say to the papers," said Mr. Sim-bold. "I mean...I am sorry about that, but I can't be respon-sible for the insane public statements of every other MEP and party member, can I? I know there's such a thing as collec-tive responsibility, but I'm really not everybody."

"If they do, at least we can use the manure as manure," said Sister Quiteria.

"Can't be worse than the seaweed," said Mr. Simbold.

"I don't see why you shouldn't use the rooms anyway. People from other parties have."

"Yes."

"I wouldn't ask if I didn't think you trustworthy," said Sis-ter Quiteria. "We would be very grateful...to both you and Ms. Thrusk."

Mr. Simbold gave her an evil eye. "What's it got to do with Ms. Thrusk?"

"Nothing," said Sister Quiteria, "at all."

Mr. Simbold eyed her suspiciously. "I'm very flattered and in principle of course I'd help you, and I'm sure Ms. Thrusk would be happy to lend a hand too if it would help."

"It wouldn't take up much of your time. I just need someone to give things a second glance...if you know what I mean. We don't want to end up spending what we haven't got. It isn't trust...it's just...if I make a mistake...financially there's never much leeway."

"I'd be glad to help," Mr. Simbold said, sounding reluctant.

"Anything you can do to help us, we will all be grateful," said Sister Quiteria, smiling. "We do hope not to impose on our guests. Our philosophy is that to enjoy the atmosphere of contemplation, the Convent offers what guests need most—privacy."

"Yes."

"And I think we offer you a lot of that, don't we?" said Sister Quiteria, placing his purchases into his Sainsbury's shopping bag very precisely. "We make sure that when you're here you're not disturbed by anybody. And that your privacy is properly respected."

"Yes.

"Except when you do your surgery...when we try to keep any protesters and troublemakers away."

"Yes."

"If, for example, you wanted to use the facilities to run any party events here, we'd be more than happy, you know. I'm sure Mother Rosalinda would be only too happy to offer a discount to your party...particularly if you've been helping us in other areas."

"Yes, Sister Quiteria. I know," said Mr. Simbold, sounding annoyed.

"I hope you don't think I'm being in any way pushy, but if we never say it, you never know."

"No. Quite. I quite understand."

"That'll be twenty pounds and a penny."

Chapter Five

One advantage of being ill, Mother Rosalinda thought, was that it seemed to give her more time to paint. Although of course she felt guilty in not participating in the more manual activities of running the guesthouse and helping with the farm, she thought she might as well be doing what she was best at while she still has time to do it. After all, she had an exhibition coming up and there was much to do and little time. She hadn't told Sister Margaret this explicitly, but they'd all been together long enough now that...well, she just knew, didn't she?

She was working on her Virgin and Child Enthroned after Domenico Veneziano, but using a mixture of cubist style and Schwitters Merz techniques. It had been demanding her attention for several weeks now. Just as she was figuring out the best way to do the Christ child's halo, Father Baines "dropped by" on his way back from helping spread the latest load of seaweed manure with Sister Maria. He smelt a bit bad, but fortunately there was a door from what Mother Rosalinda called her studio into the garden so she could talk to him without inviting him in. This helped reduce some of the pong and meant he didn't have to come in and spread muck around...around her.

"Good afternoon, Mother Rosalinda," he said. "God bless you."

Now Mother Rosalinda was religious, of course, but she had certain objections to people gratuitously stuffing God's name into everyday conversation—although she was not sure what they were. She'd never really articulated them fully, but if she had to, she'd have probably said something along the lines of using God for self-propaganda purposes rather than seeing him as a person to engage in conversation.

"Good afternoon, Father," said Mother Rosalinda, trying to not make it sound like "go away."

"How's the painting going?" said Father Baines.

"Fine," said Mother Rosalinda. "How's the muckspreading going?"

"We're getting there," said Father Baines.

"Good."

"I really wish I could do something more useful for you."

"Spreading muck is very useful," replied Mother Rosalinda, thinking, *as long as it's not on the Internet.* "I hope Sister Maria hasn't been working you too hard."

"Not at all," Father Baines said, though his tone lacked conviction. "I don't know as I'm best suited to this, though."

"Are you not?"

"When I offered, Sister Maria had said something about helping doing the accounts," said Father Baines.

"Yes, well, we had to have a bit of a reorganisation due to my condition. Sister Quiteria's looking after all that now...with the help of Mr. Simbold."

"What does Mr. Simbold do?" asked Father Baines.

"You'd have to ask Sister Quiteria that. I can't micromanage everything." She didn't like the phrase micromanage—she had picked it up off Sister Quiteria—but she felt it would annoy Father Baines, so she used it. "There has to be some devolution. I think he just helps her add up and that. I'm not sure exactly...but he is a solicitor, so we felt he might stop any legal problems before they become issues."

"Oh," said Father Baines. "None of my business, of course, but he spends a lot of time here, doesn't he?"

"So do you," replied Mother Rosalinda tartly. *No, it isn't really any of your business,* she thought.

"Yes. You don't worry, do you, about the image he gives of the convent?" said Father Baines

"You're right, Father," said Mother Rosalinda. "I don't worry. Anyway, I would have thought his conservative views were very much up your street. He supports SPUC and—"

"Well, it's true," said Father Baines, "that he's very conservative, but should we really be getting too involved with any political party?"

"We're letting him a room to sleep and work in, Father,

it's not a political endorsement...as you know. We let the other parties use the place for their surgeries if they ask...so why not him? Unless he's saying anything particularly outrageous, I don't think we can throw him out. After all, his money's as good as anyone else's, and we do need the money," said Mother Rosalinda. "I'd remind you of Matthew 7:1."

"I'm not saying he's a bad man," said Father Baines, "just that we should be careful. I'd remind you of Canon 915. We must be seen to be careful not to promote."

"We're not promoting anything."

"You might be if you allow him to hold meetings here."

"He's only doing his surgeries. Hardly advising everyone publically to have an abortion," said Mother Rosalinda. "I mean, he is pro-life. Shouldn't you like him?"

"There are other things one can do that are not what the church is aiming to promote," said Father Baines.

"If you're trying to tell me he's doing something he shouldn't be, it'd be best to say it," said Mother Rosalinda. "Or talk to your bishop about it. He is the authority in these matters, I believe. I am merely a nun."

"I was also thinking of Canon 285. We're not allowed to stand for public office, you know, and we don't want to be seen to align ourselves too closely..." Father Baines trailed off.

Father Baines always spoke as if he was the Catholic Church personally, thought Mother Rosalinda. Which was silly because, personally speaking, the Church was Christ and his Father and the Spirit. That was always how Father Baines behaved. It was so tedious. No wonder the bishop would rather have him spreading seaweed.

"That's very kind of you, Father," she said. "But I'd rather you thought about how we're going to shift the next lot of seaweed. I don't what to criticise what you've done because I am grateful, but we do need to get more out faster. Now is the optimum time." This wasn't true, but she knew Father Baines knew nothing about farming so he couldn't question it cogently and she thought it would piss him off. Mother Rosalinda enjoyed pissing off Father Baines.

"Anything you ask," said Father Baines with a mixture of sarcasm and obsequiousness, "Mother Superior. Although I do wish there was something else I could do."

"I'm sure you do," said Mother Rosalinda, trying not to laugh and thinking, *I bet you do*. "But this is, I'm afraid, what most needs to be done and it's difficult to change the rota without the others feeling they're being treated unfairly...particularly at the moment when everyone is doing more than their usual load. But you know while we always appreciate your help...well...you do know that if you don't want to help, you don't have to." She knew as well as he did that while this was literally true, it was not actually true.

"Yes, I do," said Father Baines, giving a smile that didn't reach his eyes.

Mother Rosalinda smiled too. She knew Bishop O'Flarty wasn't going to let him rant in public again for a very long time. At least not under his own name...no matter how much stinking seaweed he shifted.

"It pleases me to help you," lied Father Baines.

"Good, I'll see you later then," said Mother Rosalinda. "I've got to get on. Goodbye, Father." She shut the door. He went away sulkily. It was a lie. She was just tired. He always took it out of her. She sat down in her easy chair and put her feet up.

How was she going to keep them all together? In the past, she'd managed to hold onto her position by making them all feel individually confided in, giving them confidences that would give them confidence in her. Trust each of them with a task the others didn't know about. She wasn't sure that was how a person was supposed to run an order, but it worked for her. Not that she was that bothered about being Mother Superior, but she imagined the others doing it very badly and was not inspired with confidence by her cogitations on what cock-ups they could make. Maybe she should give up and just trust in God. Then again, she wasn't that ill...yet. Not *ill* ill. Still, she would be...

Anyway, what special task could she think of for Sister Quiteria? If she was going to continue to decline or get worse before she got better, she'd need someone to help her with some contingency planning. She sat back and began to think things out, but fell asleep only to be woken up later by the bird scarers.

Chapter Six

Bishop O'Flarty thought people had the wrong idea of what it was like to be a bishop. They thought it was all contemplation and talking quietly on "Thought for the Day," or they thought he was busy visiting parishes and supervising confirmation classes and visiting schools or something...and summoning his priests to see him when they did wrong.

In fact, it seemed to him he spent far too much time settling arguments rather than enforcing God's will. Arguments between priests. Arguments between priests and the laity. Arguments between the Latin Mass Society and the V2D2 (Vatican Two Dialog Too) group. Arguments between himself and his own priests. Arguments. Arguments. Arguments.

As to his priests, if he visited them too often, they would complain to anyone who could hear about being picked on. He also found himself not just visiting them in a planned fashion, but contriving ever more convoluted excuses to drop in on them "in passing" and thus not opening himself up to the accusation of harassing them at work/prayer. He often thought about how wonderful it would be to go on "Back to the Floor." However, it might be regarded as sacrilegious to be ordained twice, so he didn't apply. Besides which, the priesthood was so small everyone knew everyone. There was no hiding. So maybe this was why he always felt like he was spying when visiting his own priests too often. This was silly because really they were just supposed to do what he told them, but they didn't.

Today he'd used the excuse of the new Vatican directive on redesigning first Holy Communion courses in order to drop in on Father Baines. Father Baines was his usual paranoid self. In a normal industry, thought Bishop O'Flarty, he'd be able to sack people who were clearly insane, but as the priesthood was supposedly a holy vocation rather than an employment, this option was seemingly unavailable to him unless Father Baines did something that was actually breaking the rules.

While Father Baines was, in his view, a very bad priest, he did not actually violate any of the rules of the church much and as such it was impossible to laicize him. Indeed never breaking the rules some might say was exactly the problem with Father Baines. Still, at least he'd found Father Baines the smallest parish there was that he could do the least damage in. Most of the punters were extremely elderly, so the fact that Father Baines' views tended not to change when the rest of the world's had was not as much of a problem here. The predominately old population of the retirement village liked their old-fashioned priest, and if they did not, their seniority ensured that this was a problem that Old Father Time would quickly ameliorate.

Father Baines was, as Bishop O'Flarty had guessed he'd be, still livid about having been made to do some real work and having been made to stop ranting on the Internet, although at the moment, he was concealing this badly under a molecule thin layer of fake humility and feigned inner reflection.

"How are you getting on with Mother Rosalinda?" asked Bishop O'Flarty.

"I think we're getting on alright," said Father Baines.

"She says you keep complaining. That isn't the kind of help I was hoping she'd get from you."

"Well, I have been trying," he replied. "I just said to her that shifting seaweed manure was perhaps...not exactly my bag."

I'd have thought you'd be very good at spreading shit about. Bishop O'Flarty found himself trying not to voice this opinion and instead said, "Perhaps, but you must help them with what they most need, Andrew."

"Well...er," said Father Baines. "It isn't that I don't want to. It's more that...well, I just would have thought I'd have been better helping Sister Quiteria with the accounts or something more clerical, but Sister Margaret—"

"I'm sure Sister Margaret knows what she's doing," interrupted Bishop O'Flarty, raising his hand in a "fatherly" way that he liked to believe reduced confrontation. He knew full well that he hadn't the first idea what Sister Margaret was doing and, moreover, he didn't want to know.

"She seems to be inviting some strange people to stay," said Father Baines.

"They run a guesthouse. They invite all kinds of people to stay," said Bishop O'Flarty.

"Oh I know," said Father Baines with the air of a man who really had no idea, "but I was a bit worried when I saw she'd invited Mohammed Bakir to their ecumenical conference."

"There is little point in an ecumenical conference to which people of other faiths are not invited," said Bishop O'Flarty

"I know," said Father Baines.

"It is going to be a bit odd if they never invite anybody of another religion to an ecumenical conference. It wouldn't be very ecumenic," said Bishop O'Flarty. "Now I don't want to hear any more of this, Father Baines. The decision was made by the Bishop's Conference. We must attempt to engage with all different faiths. That is the purpose of the nuns running such events, and very positive and important it is too."

Father Baines straightened himself up a bit and replied. "I understand that, Bishop. I'm not disputing that...but...I have read about him."

"Who haven't you read about?"

Ignoring the question, Father Baines continued. "He may seem legitimate now, but he has a history. In the Kurdish region of Iraq where he's from...during Saddam's time, he was well known for being part of the Ba'athist—"

"That's something you must put to Mother Rosalinda. That's for her to consider," said Bishop O'Flarty.

"But you're the bishop," pointed out Father Baines. "Ultimately what happens there will reflect on you...and as I say, there were rumours that back when the Kurds were gassed, he was somehow involved in the government's—"

"Put a sock in it, Baines," Bishop O'Flarty snapped. "If you want to dream up crackpot theories, at least think them up about things you know about, like the Catechism. He's a Sunni Imam. It doesn't make him an international terrorist. He hasn't been arrested for anything, has he?"

"Not exactly."

"Has he?"

"No."

"And he's not in the papers for having done anything terrible, is he?"

"Nothing. But at least with the Dalai Lama..."

"So what's the problem?"

"The problem," said Father Baines, "isn't a problem as such. It's just that—"

"It's just that there isn't a problem," said Bishop O'Flarty, "except in your imagination where there's always a problem, isn't there?" He pointed a finger. "You're the problem, Father Baines. You're the paranoid one. That's what our psychologist said."

"It doesn't mean I'm not right and I don't have a point and that you shouldn't listen," said Father Baines. "Bishop. You can be paranoid and—"

"Don't 'Bishop' me. I'm not in the mood, Father. You just do as I tell you to do for once, and we shall all be a lot happier. I want you to help Mother Rosalinda...because she's our Sister in Christ and she's been good to us...all of us...and she's very ill and I've asked you to do it. It should be a privilege to shift their seaweed."

"Yes, Bis... Yes."

"Good, then I don't want to hear any more about it."

He didn't for quite a while.

Chapter Seven

Mr. Simbold of the United Kingdom Independence Party was not having a good time. His drive for more ethnic minority members after initially hitting the brick wall that there wasn't much of an ethnic minority in many of the local rural communities had seemed to turn up trumps at last. He had managed to recruit a large number local Tamils. Unfortunately, what he hadn't realised was that they were rather keen members of the Liberation Tigers of Tamil Eelam (LTTE) and their motivation had been largely entryism. Of course, not all the Tamils were members of the LTTE...some were good honest UKIPers. Nevertheless, the local press had had a field day insinuating that he was in cahoots with a so-called "terrorist" organisation. Mr. Simbold pointed out patiently that the LTTE wasn't a proscribed organisation within the United Kingdom, which far from quietened the situation. It enraged the Sri Lankan High Commissioner and pushed the story from local news to low-grade national scandal. The public image of the local party took a further battering when it transpired that the local party's accounts showed it mysteriously lacking in money that should have been there.

The upshot of all this was that there would be another internal party inquiry. Mr. Simbold started to worry they might start to ask more questions about how much he had been paying his secretary. Not that there was exactly a great deal of financial impropriety, but there might be some adultery. Not that Mr. Simbold thought he was an adulterer. He wasn't even that religious, but the Convent was ideally situated for his needs being near to where his secretary Angelaika lived...so he went along with it. He didn't actually have sex there. He just slept there and went round to her place...most of the time. They couldn't do it very well on the nun's beds anyway. Besides, as far as he was concerned, his wife had cheated on him many times. Their marriage had long been a sham, and he was a grown man who had every right to get his end away. While this might not be following the Catholic faith to the letter, he was sure God didn't mind too much so long as he didn't take communion. Of course, he did take communion, but this was to keep up appearances not because he wanted to. If he didn't, people might ask questions and there would be gossip, but he was sure God understood all that. God was very understanding.

As usual, Sister Quiteria had dragged him into administrative matters as soon as his constituency surgery was over. She wasn't a bad-looking girl, he imagined...from what he saw of her. She had a nice face. He couldn't tell what they all looked like all over or the shape of all of them, but some were clearly not spring chickens. He wondered if her asking him if he would help her with the accounting was a pretence for getting closer. He dismissed the idea. It would be too much like something out of a trashy novel.

One day, he was helping her with the EU paperwork and they happened to get onto what the land the nuns owned was actually worth.

"What do you mean what's it worth?" asked Mr. Simbold.

"Well, the whole thing, I suppose. The farm, the house, the guesthouse, the chapel...the whole place," replied Sister Quiteria.

"Isn't that a bit of an earthly question?" teased Mr. Simbold.

"Well, it's a practical question," said Sister Quiteria. "You know we may have to sell or move some time."

"Really?" said Mr. Simbold. "Surely not in the immediate future?"

"Well, it's no secret," said Sister Quiteria, "that we sometimes have a lot of difficulty breaking even and that we rely in no small part on the sale of Mother Rosalinda's art."

"But surely that's very cynical? Not very Godly?"

"I know what you're saying, Mr. Simbold," she said, "but it's up to God when he takes each of us and I'm sure God would want us to plan for the future. If he literally told us what to do all the time. there'd be no part for us to play, would there?"

"I suppose not."

"Of course the Mother House would help us out if it turned out we hit a sudden financial shortfall—that is after all how we moved here in the first place...but nevertheless, we do have to think if staying here is the best way to pursue our mission."

"I think it is," said Mr. Simbold.

"That's because it's convenient for you," said Sister Quiteria. Mr. Simbold thought this slightly rude. She continued. "I don't mean that in a nasty way. We all seek out what is easy. It is a beautiful and historical place here, but you must remember we didn't go into a Convent in order to own things, including the buildings themselves."

Mr. Simbold gave her a look as if to say, "*Are you having me on?*"

Sister Quiteria gave Mr. Simbold a look as if to say, "*Don't be stupid. I'm a nun.*"

"All I'm asking is...could you make some enquiries?"

"Some enquiries?"

"About potentially selling the building and grounds and what it would be worth on the open market. I know it may seem an odd request, but Mother Rosalinda would be very grateful. The thing is, you see, we don't want to start a rumour in the village or in the press...so things need to be tackled with some tact and diplomacy."

"And you think I have those qualities?" said Mr. Simbold.

"Well, you are a politician. Aren't you supposed to have them?" said Sister Quiteria. "And you are a solicitor, so technically you'd know the paperwork if and when we decide to sell."

"Well, you can sell without a solicitor these days," said Mr. Simbold. "What you can't do is sell without publicity. The moment you go to an estate agent, people will know it's on the market."

Sister Quiteria smiled. "We may not be planning to sell the place to just any bidder. We may already have another buyer in mind...another religious community. With more members. The question then is knowing a fair price. In which case we'd need someone to give us a fair valuation and to arrange exchange of contracts. In my experience, a lot of things that seem complicated can be made much simpler...so long as you have the right kind of help. Can't they?"

"I suppose so," said Mr. Simbold.

"Just keep it under your hat a bit. And we'll keep things..."

"Beneath your veils?"

"Exactly. Now then, tea?"

Just then Father Baines ran into the room without knocking. Mr. Simbold was pissed off. Baines had only just gone back out in the fields instead of hanging round the shop skiving and moaning how he was better than the manure that covered his boots. Mr. Simbold was about to remonstrate with him for not knocking when he looked at him again. He was muddy top to bottom—he had obviously fallen over. There was blood down his arm...but his coat was not torn. It was not his blood. He was whiter than expected, even in the cutting wind outside.

"Come quick!" he shouted. "And call an ambulance."

Chapter Eight

There was no point in calling an ambulance. Sister Margaret was dead when they got there. How exactly was hard to say, but she'd clearly disconnected the muck spreader because there was a problem with the tractor's PTO shaft, and somehow, she had become entangled in the spinning shaft after removing the cover. When exactly she died was not clear. She could have died any time in the previous two hours. No one had heard her scream. Perhaps it happened too quickly for her to scream, or perhaps no one could hear her scream from the middle of the field.

Later, the pathologist guessed she was knocked out quickly. She had been spun many times before falling off. Her clothes were torn and bones had been snapped by the force of the rotation. Her head was smashed in. It was a fairly horrific and unpleasant way to die.

It was unpleasant too for Father Baines, who found the body, and Sister Quiteria and Mr. Simbold, who he seemed to insist on dragging to stare at it as if they could do anything. Neither did Mother Rosalinda, who eventually had to identify the body enjoy the scene.

"Horrible," said Mr. Simbold, feeling physically sick and as though he was understating the problem.

"Yes," said Sister Quiteria.

"We should say a prayer," said Father Baines.

"Bit late for that now," said Mr. Simbold and then felt guilty straight away.

Father Baines eyed him darkly. His eyes said, "For her soul."

"Yes, of course," said Mr. Simbold, feeling shame...an emotion he didn't feel often.

They said the Lord's prayer while they waited for the ambulance to arrive and then started on a Hail Mary. The field was muddy. The wind was cutting mercilessly through their clothes.

Mother Rosalinda was quick on the scene despite her increasing infirmity. She was shortly followed by Doctor Fay Bones who, as it happened, had been visiting her. An ambulance turned up soon after. Doctor Fay Bones felt her cold body to check she was fully dead and said she must have died instantly.

Mother Rosalinda was distraught. "It's my fault," she told Sister Quiteria.

"It isn't anyone's fault," said Sister Quiteria. "It's an accident. It could have happened to any of us."

"It is my fault," said Mother Rosalinda, "and you're wrong...it couldn't. I should never have asked Margaret to do the muck spreading. I knew she was hopeless with machinery."

"So did we," said Sister Quiteria, "but you can't blame yourself."

"I am to blame."

"It looks like there was something wrong with the shaft guard. You shouldn't be able to do that," said Father Baines, although it seemed no one quite understood what he was explaining.

"She's removed the guard," said Mother Rosalinda. "Probably it wasn't working properly and—"

"That's because there was something wrong with it...obviously," said Father Baines.

"Why is it obvious?" asked Mother Rosalinda.

"Is it obvious?" said Quiteria.

They all looked at the bloodied PTO shaft, mangled guard, and tangled clothes, but no one could answer the point. It was impossible to know what really happened without being an expert in forensic science, but Sister Quiteria's theory that it was just a horrific accident was comforting...even if it wasn't true...or might be true. She seemed to believe it.

"We'll probably have no way of knowing what really happened," said Doctor Fay Bones, coming over and overcoming his usual reticence towards any human interaction. "Sadly, these accidents are all too common on farms. It doesn't matter how well people know that they shouldn't go near the PTO shaft, should stand back from it at all times even when it's not powered up, and keep the guard up... It's just...one of those things...like hitting a pedestrian. It can happen at any time. You think it's safe, but you've only got to lose your concentration for a moment and... You mustn't blame yourself, Mother Rosalinda." He touched her arm.

"Yes," said Mother Rosalinda, "but I knew she was cack handed and still insisted she did it. She didn't want to work in the fields. She told me she was no good at it. We all knew she wasn't." Mother Rosalinda and Sister Margaret had been very close. Sister Margaret had been her right hand woman.

For once, Father Baines managed to think about something else instead of internal church arguments. He tried to offer spiritual comfort to the woman who didn't like him even though she didn't seem to want it. "Mother Rosalinda," said Father Baines, "you can't blame yourself for this. You've had enough troubles. You've been very ill yourself and on medication. You can't think of everything...it's not possible...to anticipate everything."

"No, it isn't," assured Doctor Fay Bones.

"All the same, if I'd have stood down as Mother Superior..."

"Then in all likelihood Sister Margaret would have sent someone else to spread seaweed in the field and...and she'd be the one racked with guilt instead of you...or still dead," said Sister Quiteria, "or something...but it wouldn't be her fault and it isn't your fault either. It was an accident. There's such a thing as survivor's syndrome, you know? You think you could have prevented it, but believe me you couldn't have prevented it."

"I know," said Mother Rosalinda. "But it just doesn't seem real, does it?"

As if to underline this point, two ambulance men walked by carrying a stretcher on which to load the crumpled corpse of Sister Margaret.

Sister Quiteria's eyes shifted to a police car some way off.

"Wait!" said a voice. A fat man in an off the peg suit and old snorkel parka seemed to have appeared from nowhere. He was trudging awkwardly over the field in footwear that was not ideal for the condition and his combover was waving in the breeze. "Detective Inspector Vail," he said, flashing a warrant card in a way he'd borrowed off Christopher Ellison.

"What?" said Mother Rosalinda.

"We need to look at the scene. Just routine," said Detective Inspector Vale.

"You don't think there's anything wrong?" asked Father Baines.

Detective Inspector Vale looked at him as if wondering why he'd asked the question.

Doctor Fay Bones said, "I think we'd better leave the Detective Inspector to do his job, Mother Rosalinda. They have to follow procedure in any sudden and unexplained death. Let me walk you back to the Convent."

"Yes," said Mother Rosalinda.

Mother Rosalinda and Doctor Fay Bones walked back to the house followed by Sister Quiteria.

"Father," Sister Quiteria heard DCI Vale inquire, "could you remain a moment, sir? I realise you may be upset, and I'm sorry to bother you so soon after...well...but...sorry...er... Could you just answer a few basic questions for me? You were the one who found the body and reported it as I understand?"

"Yes," said Father Baines.

"Good. I have a few questions. Just routine. We have to go through the official motions. I'm sure you understand. Detective Constable Bland, I wonder..."

Doctor Fay Bones, Mother Rosalinda, and Sister Quiteria were out of earshot now. Sister Quiteria looked back over her shoulder. A small army of men in police uniforms and white overalls seemed to have emerged from nowhere (or the local countryside...which was arguably the same) and were busy sticking white poles in the ground and measuring and photographing everything from every angle.

A smaller coagulation of men in ill-fitting business suits had also materialised, but what their function was except to stand around trying to look hard in knee-length overcoats was more opaque.

Chapter Nine

Detective Inspector Vale was unhappy about the death of Sister Maria. Well, that was to say he was happy to have a potential murder to investigate—very little criminal activity happened in the locality—but unhappy about the situation. He'd read the various manuals on potential homicides and, of course, he'd been involved in homicide and accident investigations in the past, but this one didn't seem to be covered in any way either by his own experience or any manual.

Of course, on the surface, it seemed like an accident. There was no motive. Who'd want to kill a nun? Other nuns? There was no theft. Indeed there was very little at the Convent to steal given the Benedictine vow of poverty. The most obvious suspect was, of course, the first on the scene—Father Baines. However, there was little to be gleaned from him...except perhaps that the man was a chronic bore and a massive bigot. House to house enquiries were fruitless as there weren't many houses near to the field or the Convent which could have seen what was going on. It was all very well, manuals saying, "*Where death or serious injury is reported or the circumstances of an incident appear suspicious, call handlers should always think murder*". But there just wasn't any real evidence of murder. It was all very well saying, "*Find out how a person lived and you will find out how they died.*" But all Detective Inspector Vale found out was that being a nun was, as he suspected, very boring. It involved a lot of praying, mass, manual labour, and talking to God. So after interviewing everybody at more length than was necessary and stacking up more overtime than was felt necessary by his boss, he and his detective constable concluded that they'd have to stop investigating altogether and passed matters on to the local coroner.

The whole inquest process took about three months. Three months of everybody answering the same stupid questions. The coroner, Ms Boothington, a white middle-aged woman with a prim air of efficiency was meticulous in going through the motions, and there was a decent turnout for the nearest thing to live entertainment that the village and the local press had encountered since the last Christmas panto. The star turn was sister Margaret's brother Mr Edward Ward who lived in the village and was the farmer down the road who kept financially undercutting them. Mother Rosalinda had known this and so had some of the other nuns...but not Sister Quiteria...she was still too new.

This proximity of Mr. Ward to his sister's address was not, it transpired, an accident. Mr. Ward was an atheist. Indeed a militant atheist. Not just the average kind of militant atheist either, but the kind of militant atheist who made Richard Dawkins look a bit wet.

Sister Margaret and Edmund had grown up in an atheist home...which was unusual in the 1950s. Their father had been killed in the last year of the Second World War, aged 21, and their mother had decided that if there was a God, she'd pretty much had enough of him and she wasn't going to have anything to do with him or have anything about him in the house. At least one of her children was infected fully with these beliefs while the other rebelled and rejected them entirely.

In short, Sister Margaret (originally Daisy before changing her name) was a convert to "the faith" while Edmund was vehemently unconverted. He knew what was expected. He should just let his sister go into a convent and become a non-person with a changed name...but believing vehemently that all religion was some kind of brainwashing after his mother's death, he sold the family farm in Yorkshire and decided to buy the farm next door to the convent. He did this partly as it was on the market anyway, but partly because he thought it would allow him an interesting means by which to damage the nuns financially and vaguely harass them. He could also make a mockery of his sister's desire to reject the society of man for Jesus's society by popping up round the estate at odd moments when Jesus and Mother Rosalinda weren't expecting him and encouraging inhabitants of the village to utilise the many rights of way the nuns used to plough over as assiduously as possible.

As Sister Margaret wasn't going to try and get her own brother arrested for stalking, the rest of the nuns just had to put up with it. Yes, indeed, he really took it all that far.

If this sounds eccentric behaviour...it was...but in his defence, he'd had other reasons for moving at the time, and he couldn't resist the chance to constantly get on that cow Mother Rosalinda's nerves. Complete hypocrite she was, claiming she wanted a life of contemplation while seeming to always get her arse on television or photographed chatting with the Palin brothers.

To cut a long story short, Edmund Ward had some slight problems and believed his sister had been murdered and spun this story very loudly to the local media. Actually what he said was he believed she had probably been driven to suicide by the depressing nature of her existence and "all those Hail Marys", but after discovering that the word "murder" tended to get into the paper more, he kept spouting it at regular intervals on the Internet and radio phone in programs and to the local hacks until his unsubstantiated allegations floated up to the nationals who loved the story of a celebrity nun killing other nuns even if it wasn't true.

Fortunately the nuns didn't have a television, but the presence of peeping photographers popping out from every bush or over the wall eventually became rather irritating. Particularly annoying was the effect on Mr. Simbold who said he really might have to stop having party meetings and surgeries in their facilities...given that the whole point of his being there was to get away from all the press. His secretary wasn't happy either as it had the potential to make their affair a rather less clandestine one than it already was...which was not very clandestine at all.

"We'll lose money if he goes," warned Sister Quiteria.

"Don't worry, it will all blow over," said Mother Rosalinda, thinking that these events were doing little to help her reserve of energy for her fight against cancer or complete the preparations for her next and potentially final exhibition.

It didn't blow over exactly, but it did blow up and out. Fortunately, Mr. Ward made himself look rather silly by his uncalled for and unrequested rants during the inquest. The coroner, Ms. Boothington, made Mr. Ward look very irrational with very little mental effort. Whether he really believed the nuns had intentionally murdered Sister Margaret or whether it was just a mixture of grief, rage, and rubbing their noses in it because no one could quite say—including psychiatrists and himself. Ms. Boothington recorded a verdict of accidental death.

However, just as they thought it was all over and were leaving the inquest, Mr. Ward cornered Mother Rosalinda again on the pavement outside beside some TV journalists and shouted, "Murderer! She'd still be alive if you spent as much time servicing your machinery as you do in your stupid services!"

Things seemed to calm down a bit after that...after all, there's only so many murdering nun puns the tabloids can do. But a couple of weeks later, an envelope came from a solicitor. It was Edmund threatening to sue them for negligence...more out of a sense of amusement than justice, but perhaps that too. Still, it did put the wind up Mother Rosalinda. "I hope he isn't serious." She sighed at the next planning meeting.

"Well, he sent it through a solicitor. Must have cost him some money," said Sister Quiteria, "but don't worry. I don't think it's serious. And I got Mr. Simbold to do a bit of an audit of our physical and financial assets...so, if it comes to it, we've got—"

"Why?" asked Mother Rosalinda, abruptly wondering how it was Sister Quiteria had ended up doing so much of what had been Sister Margaret's job.

"Just a sensible precaution," said Sister Quiteria. "After all, we don't know what's going to happen."

The other nuns looked at her blankly.

"Look at the birds of the air, Sister Quiteria, they do not sow or reap or store away in barns," said Mother Rosalinda enigmatically. They all looked out the window. There were no birds, just the sounds of bird scarers.

"I still can't believe she's dead," said Sister Maria. "She was always so careful."

"As Doctor Fay Bones said, it can happen to anyone," said Sister Quiteria. No one was completely convinced.

Chapter Ten

"It's bollocks," said Edmund to Detective Inspector Vale for the fourteenth time.

"Perhaps," said Detective Inspector Vale who was now beyond giving Edmund that look that said, *You realise you are swearing in front of a police officer.* "But there is no proof of foul play so the coroner has to return that verdict. I'm afraid that unless we can turn up more evidence, then this is...well, the end of the line." Detective Inspector Vale hated victim support. In Detective Inspector Vale's view, his job was to catch criminals, and all this pussyfooting around listening to "victims" wasn't what he'd joined the force for.

After all, Edmund Ward wasn't really a victim. He was actually a man who just imagined himself as a victim because he was bereaved. It was sad. It was unfortunate. That said, loads of people were bereaved. It didn't mean they were entitled to be an endless drain on his time. *Really what's happening,* he thought, *is that people like me who are supposed to be busy upholding the law are actually being used as social workers.* It wasn't a very sensible use of his time because he was paid more than a social worker.

"The thing is, Mr. Ward," he said, "we have to look at these things in terms of practicalities: the seriousness of the offence and the likelihood of solvability versus the level of resources. We don't know that an offence has even taken place, and without knowing even that we can't begin to hope to solve it. In the meantime, it's eating up our resources. I know to you that might sound dreadfully cynical, but the criminal justice system doesn't deliver perfect justice. It just delivers some justice where there's the evidence to deliver it. I know that's disappointing for you, but sometimes we just have to face it that the evidence isn't there. I was cut up on the roundabout last year, but I still had to go 50:50 with the insurance company because I couldn't prove it was the other driver's fault...and I'm a policeman. I realise that's a very tactless analogy and you've suffered a great deal more than I did, but that's..." He sighed.

Edmund sat back in the police station plastic chair, picked a large bogey from his nose, placed it in his mouth, and chewed it slowly, savouring it as if it was a tasty treat.

Detective Inspector Vale was unsure if this was a satirical observation of some kind or he just liked eating bogies. He suspected both.

"Are you," said Edmund after a minute or so, "comparing my sister's murder to bumping your car?"

"No," said Detective Inspector Vale, "and we don't know it's murder. It may be murder, but as I say...what evidence is there? I can see no motive. I've looked at all the suspects."—*Including you*, he thought, but didn't say. "And there just isn't any to be found. I've looked at the evidence...if anything, it does support the coroner's theory that this was accidental death."

"It was murder."

"It's possible it was manslaughter or criminal negligence," said Detective Inspector Vale, "but in my opinion...and it is my professional opinion...this isn't murder."

"Manslaughter?"

"That's often harder to prove than murder," said Detective Inspector Vale.

"I still think it was murder."

"Even if it was manslaughter, I think we'd have a hard time getting a group of nuns convicted for a lack of corporate responsibility," said Detective Inspector Vale. "They're a religious order, not I.C.I."

"Why?"

"Well, you'd have to prove gross negligence," said Detective Inspector Vale. "Not just that they were negligent, but that they were seriously negligent. You'd need to sell that to a jury. I mean, you could try a priva—"

"—who are likely to be sympathetic because the public are sentimental about nuns?"

"That's not quite how I'd put it," said Detective Inspector

Vale, "but it is a point to consider."

"A point to consider" was one of Detective Inspector Vale's catchphrases. It meant "*I'm listening to you because I have to and not because I actually give a shit.*"

Detective Inspector Vale lifted his hands in the air and put them behind his head and leant back in the chair. He scratched at his combover and put his hands down again. "We have to ask ourselves if there is a realistic chance of prosecuting anybody, and I don't think there is. They're a religious community, not a business. If it was someone like—"

"That bitch Mother Rosalinda, doesn't she have a duty of care?" said Edmund.

"Well, yes, but given your publically stated vendetta against the order, people might think your own motivation...and I'd prefer it that you didn't use that word in my station..."

"What's my motivation got to do with anything?" said Edmund.

Detective Inspector Vale was going to say "nothing" when he stopped and thought to himself...*actually, what is your motivation?* Even given his atheism, wasn't it a bit odd that Edmund Ward was this determined to cause so much trouble for the nuns? Wasn't it odder that he'd gone to the bother of buying the farm next door? Detective Inspector Vale had tried to "think murder" about this subject before. He thought about it again, but as before, he was afraid he got nowhere...or not much farther. His suspicious cogitations left an ominous silence.

"I don't have a vendetta," said Edmund Ward to break the silence, "but I do think my sister was murdered. Not died accidentally. Not the victim of some horrible cock-up. Not an accident statistic. I think she was murdered. And I think it because, looking at the alternatives, they don't add up. She might not have been good with farm machinery, but she was never clumsy. And she might have been stupid, but she wasn't retarded. And she might have been a bit mad, but she wasn't depressed. So why would she end up wrapped around the PTO shaft? Sherlock Holmes said that when you eliminate the impossible, whatever remains, however improbable, must be the truth. Well, I've eliminated the other alternatives because they don't add up to what I know about my sister, and I'm telling you she was murdered."

"Yes, sir," said Detective Inspector Vale wearily. "Sherlock Holmes did indeed say that, and that's why Lestrade wouldn't have had him for a policeman. I'm sorry, but the facts are these...I'm not Sherlock Holmes. I'm paid for by the taxpayer. We found no evidence of foul play. Neither did the coroner. So this is a cold case. If you don't like that, you have every right to hire a P.I. like Sherlock...but I'd advise you not to. It's such a cold case that it's frozen solid, because there is no trail to follow...and the reason there is no trail to follow? If you ask me, there is no crime. That's my professional advice. I cannot help you any longer, and I'm afraid I'm going to have to ask you to leave now."

Chapter Eleven

The death of Sister Margaret created more problems in the logistics of the community. For a start, all the tasks had to be redistributed again. Previously, Sister Margaret had been in charge of drawing up rotas. She had not shared much of her knowledge with anyone, so no one quite understood how she had done it. This made drawing up any new rotas much more time-consuming, so the job was passed on to Sister Quiteria.

It occurred to Sister Quiteria that this should probably be Mother Rosalinda's job as the head of the community, but Mother Rosalinda didn't like doing it, so she had previously delegated it to Sister Margaret. This meant that if there were any complaints or moans, these were directed to Sister Margaret rather than Mother Rosalinda...in the same way that when Sister Margaret had been a Head Teacher, she had employed a Deputy Head Teacher to do all the unpleasant tasks with regards to discipline that she would rather not sully herself with as they were by their nature unpleasant. Mother Rosalinda used to pretend effectively to the other nuns to be above their politics this way, but of course she was very intimately involved in every decision—just at a discrete distance.

Almost inevitably as a result of the death of Sister Margaret, eventually Sister Quiteria seemed to find herself taking on more and more of the roles Sister Margaret had while retaining her existing positions in charge of accounts and the shop. Not that Mother Rosalinda particularly favoured Sister Quiteria or liked or trusted her...there just wasn't that much choice. There were only fifteen of them after all and many of the older nuns had health problems. One or two were senile.

Sister Carmelina and Sister Luciana were Italian speakers who had come over during the war and still seemed to have problems with English after fifty years. Other Sisters were either too bossy or not interested or avoidant of responsibility to be given any real authority. And Sister Maria couldn't really be trusted with any meaningful responsibility at the moment as she was under censure by the Vatican for her book, *Il lato femminile di Cristo.*

On the plus side, being "censored" by the Vatican had made Sister Maria's book something of a best seller on Amazon, providing them with some much needed income. On the downside, an investigation by the Congregation for the Doctrine of the Faith had branded the book full of "radical feminist themes incompatible with the Catholic faith." This is why the Mother House had sent Sister Maria to England. Someone at the Vatican had the vague hope that the book would not be translated into too many languages by the publisher. Unfortunately for the church but fortunately for their bank balance, the publisher refused to pull the work and even found a clause in their contract that allowed them to print a second edition with a controversial preface by Hans Küng. To be fair to the Vatican, the book didn't so much veer away from traditional Catholic teachings as perform a remarkable number of theological U-turns and mental gymnastics, so Sister Maria supposed that they were "just doing their job" by censoring her.

Sister Quiteria now seemed to be spending more and more time managing the guest house and in the shop, which she didn't mind as much now that the head of accounts (Sister Quiteria) had decided it was a sensible expenditure to put a heater fan in.

Mother Rosalinda didn't monitor her spending too carefully these days as she was spending ever more time either sleeping or working on her upcoming exhibition. Fred, her dealer, was sure it would be a huge success—particularly after her interview in the Sunday Times with the Palin Brothers who had made her on trend again by buying some of her religious paintings and making them both more sexual and sacrilegious by "satirically" appending sex toys with superglue to some of them. The interviewer had asked Mother Rosalinda what she thought of this, and Mother Rosalinda had said diplomatically that obviously as a nun she did not approve, but she had nothing against the Palin Brothers "as people."

"Were they friends?" the interviewer had asked.

Mother Rosalinda had pointed out that technically she was in an enclosed order and the interviewer thought better of asking "*Why do you seem to do so many media interviews then?*" because she couldn't quite put her finger on why this might be a contradiction. Anyway, a person shouldn't pick on people who may be potentially terminally ill.

Fred actually found her illness was another great sales angle for the exhibition. "May be your last chance to buy cheaply," he would tell people and "Bound to shoot up in price after she's dead." He did not tell Mother Rosalinda this, of course. It wasn't that agents, dealers, and promoters hated anyone living. It was just that in many ways, the dead were often the best clients. Although they didn't produce any more work to sell, they didn't chase him for royalties either or complain that he was not selling their stuff for enough. So it was swings and roundabouts.

The upshot of the new rota was that Sister Maria seemed to end up spending even more time on the tractor and around the farm doing jobs she disliked than she used to. In her cell, she sometimes felt alone with God or with herself, but outside it, she felt a kind of loneliness one can only feel in the wide and open. A feeling that someone or something was going to steal up on her even though she knew she was the only person there.

As if to make her feel more uncomfortable, she would sometimes be "helped" by Father Baines. At the moment, he was helping her with silage. Sister Maria knew the police had been very suspicious of Father Baines and these suspicions, although she knew them to be unfounded, couldn't help but affect her attitude towards him. It had always been negative, but was now paranoid and negative. When she was operating the forage harvester and he came near, she would always be careful to switch off the engine before he got too close—although she knew nothing was going to happen. It wouldn't have been so bad if he didn't try and force his opinions on her all the time. For example, one day when they were covering one of the silage clamps with black sheets, he started on about some Imam called Bakir who was attending the Ecumenical Conference.

"He's got a terrible reputation in Iraq," he said.

"Who hasn't?" said Sister Maria, thinking *I haven't exactly got the best reputation myself.* Then, she curiously asked, "What for?"

"It was rumoured he was involved in Saddam's WMD program."

"How?"

"I'm not sure exactly. I've tried reading about it, but my Arabic isn't—"

"But you brought it up, Father. You must have more reason than that to be suspicious of him?"

"I'm suspicious of the whole thing. Ecumenical Conferences—any excuse for watering down the faith. Why do we want to talk to the Dalai Lama?"

"It's just a lot of boring old men talking," said Sister Maria. "And Mother Rosalinda and some of the others. And it makes money. What harm can it do just to talk?"

"I thought you were all supposed to be here to pray?"

"It's not a silent order," said Sister Maria. "Mind you, odd stuff goes on here, doesn't it?"

"Meaning?"

"Well, Sister Margaret," said Sister Maria. "Do you really think that was an accident?"

"The coroner thought it was an accident, and I agree with the coroner. Why don't you?"

"Probably for the same reason that you think Imam Bakir is up to no good."

"That's not the same."

"Isn't it? You know when you just know something is wrong?"

"No," said Father Baines, "my suspicions are usually based on facts."

"Well, I know there's something wrong about the death of Sister Margaret. Edmund Ward knew it too."

"Edmund Ward doesn't know anything," Father Baines corrected her sternly. "He's a sad, paranoid man who hates organised religion and is upset that his sister's dead."

"I knew her. She wasn't like that. She wasn't good with machines, but she didn't take risks."

"Close, were you?"

"We're not allowed to be too close to each other," said Sister Maria, neatly sidestepping the question. "I believe there's something wrong for the same reason that you believe there's something wrong with your Imam Bakir. It doesn't add up."

"Let it go," said Father Baines.

"I will if you will."

"Perhaps," said Father Baines, which meant *yes, you will and I won't*. "Let's get on with the job, shall we?"

"Yes," said Sister Maria, still trying to evaluate how much practical help Father Baines actually was. It wasn't a lot, but she supposed he was better than nothing.

Chapter Twelve

Simon Simbold's secretary Angelaika Thrusk had the hump with him. Simon was too tired to make love again. She could force him to take a tablet, but what was the point? She wanted to be wanted. Instead, he made her feel slotted in. "This is stupid," she said. "You book a room over there and then you spend all your time at mine."

"I have to keep up appearances," said Simon Simbold.

"Why? We're together all the time anyway at functions and at the parliament and at party meetings. It surely isn't a secret to anybody. I'm pretty sure the whole village knows. Everyone's known for ages that you and your wife are separated. What's the point?"

Mr. Simbold looked at her. Her breasts were not covered by the duvet. He looked around the room. It was a rented flat. The carpet was green. The walls were white. The collection of knickknacks passing themselves off as ornaments was revolting. The smoke from her cigarette made strange patterns in the shaft of light that came through the crack in the curtains. It was undoubtedly the most interesting thing in the room.

"I'm a public figure."

"No one cares."

"They do. They just don't say it."

"You're just scared of your wife."

"Anyone who isn't scared of my wife," said Mr. Simbold, "hasn't met her."

"I think you like the nuns."

"Well, of course I like them or I wouldn't use the place—"

"I think you fancy some of them. That Quiteria one you hang out with..."

"Yes, well, you needn't worry about her. They're moving soon."

"Moving?" said Angelaika. "Why would they be moving?"

"Because...they're not making enough money, I suppose," said Mr. Simbold.

Angelaika looked at him. She looked him up and down. He was fat and middle-aged and without his suit on, he was even less to look at than he was when she drove him everywhere. He was a pillock, she thought. The word was fairly new to her, but she picked it up recently and decided she really liked it. It fit Simon Simbold. It was what he was. A man who thought he was "it," but was actually just a bit shit. He didn't even have the distinction of being amusingly bad at what he did like his deputy Mr. McWilliams, whose actions he always had to apologise to the press for. People just played him. She was playing him. "You're an idiot," she said.

"I'm not," said Mr. Simbold.

"Why would they sell then?" she asked.

"I don't know," said Mr. Simbold. "But they asked me if I'd help them handle the sale of the property discretely."

"Why discretely?"

"In case it doesn't happen, I suppose. They've got a buyer lined up. Someone's made some kind of offer on the property. Some kind of Buddhist order."

"What are they going to do with it?"

"Turn it into a different kind of...religious place, I suppose. I don't know."

"What do you mean you don't know? You're helping them...why are you helping them?"

"Why not?"

Angelaika laughed. She knew Simon was really up to something no good when he professed to be doing something for altruistic reasons. "Isn't it enough you rent rooms from them? If it was a Travelodge, you wouldn't be doing their conveyancing and stuff for free."

"It's really not that difficult."

"Are you worried they will blackmail you?"

"No."

"You needn't be...like I say, no one's actually interested in your life. Darling," she said, putting a hand on his knee and smiling sarcastically, "you're not in the government. No one cares what you do."

"I'm an MEP," protested Mr. Simbold. "And we're the second largest UK party in the European Parliament. So people do care...what we get up to. The Tamils do anyway. Why do you work for me and the party if you don't think we're important?"

"Why do you stay in a convent when you don't believe in God?"

"How do you know I don't believe in God?"

"I know you," she said...although she knew she didn't really know or care whether he believed in God. It was just good fun pressing all his buttons. There was something terribly sexy about a pompous man.

"I'm just a good Catholic. That's why I stay there and that's why I use the place and that's why I help them with things...from time to time...which are not too difficult for me but would be expensive if they had to pay someone else for them."

"You stay there because it's cheap."

"I do not."

"And you're cheap."

"I am not."

"Of course not, darling," said Angelaika. "It's okay. I'm not jealous of your nuns."

"Good."

"But I still don't understand why we have to keep everything so secret. I'm sure your wife knows you screw around...and she screws around."

"Because we do. I've got children," said Mr. Simbold.

"Anyway, if you ask me, there's something else wrong there."

"What?"

"Well, there just is...isn't there?"

"You mean Sister Margaret?"

"I mean the whole thing. The whole place."

"But what exactly?"

"I don't know..."

"So you're just guessing?"

"You're the politician. Are you seriously telling me you don't feel anything's wrong?"

"I don't know," said Mr. Simbold. "I don't think so."

"Don't worry your pretty little head about it," said Angelaika. She put her cigarette out.

Chapter Thirteen

Mother Rosalinda was having one of her worse days. She was still not too noticeably ill most of the time, but she had just had another round of chemotherapy. After six hours of being connected to a drip, she'd been driven back from the hospital by Sister Quiteria in the vomit yellow Austin Allegro. It was an unfortunate choice of colour as it made her feel like she wanted to vomit. Later, she did.

After a lie down in her cell, she'd then taken a turn for the worse. This was not unusual. First the vomiting and then the dizziness. Sister Quiteria brought her some soup to see if she could keep anything down, but honestly, everything either made her want to throw up or tasted like it was made from aluminium.

Doctor Ronald Fay Bones said this was actually quite a normal reaction and had prescribed her something for it, but on the way back from the bathroom, she collapsed again. Only momentarily, but it made her and the other nuns very scared when Sister Maria heard her thud onto the floor. Sister Maria suggested calling an ambulance, but Mother Rosalinda, not wanting to go back to hospital, said she was alright. She hated the hospital.

Sister Quiteria called Doctor Fay Bones again.

Doctor Fay Bones seemed worried, but not unduly. "It's probably just a side effect of the chemotherapy," he said as he walked back to his car. *He always says something like that,* thought Sister Quiteria, but then he added, "It's all very odd, isn't it?"

"Is it?" said Sister Quiteria. "I'm not a doctor so I wouldn't know...what's odd and what isn't." She felt guilty that they were talking behind Mother Rosalinda's back. Why doctors felt the need to talk about their patients to people who weren't the patient was beyond Sister Quiteria. She felt like pointing out that Mother Rosalinda and she were both grown women, and she was not in loco parentis, but this was not her greatest concern.

"Well," said Doctor Fay Bones, "I don't want to alarm you...or anyone, but I've been thinking about some of her symptoms..." He trailed off.

"She's got cancer," interjected Sister Quiteria, "like you said. What symptoms did you expect? I mean...that is...you told us..."

"Yes, but..." Doctor Fay Bones pulled at his collar. "I've been looking back over her case notes recently, and it set me wondering. It's just an outside theory, mind, but... It's my job to consider everything, isn't it? Sorry. I shouldn't have said anything."

"If you need to talk about it, you can talk to me," said Sister Quiteria. "Shall we go for a walk?" She added this in a tone that meant *"If there's something you don't want the others to hear, maybe we should go that way."*

"Yes," said Doctor Fay Bones, and they walked out the cloister door into the grounds together. "I mean...and tell me if you think this is too farfetched...at any point. I'd...sort of put it to the back of my mind...but then Father Baines kept on at me about foul play...so perhaps it's paranoia...but then Sister Maria did too...with another mad theory...I mean, I know they're both into mad conspiracy theories and that, but...so...you understand I may be just irrationally trying to rationalise what people have put to me?"

"Doctor Fay Bones," said Sister Quiteria in an insistent voice.

"Yes," said the doctor.

"You're a very logical man...and I know you. And I know you wouldn't voice any wild accusations that weren't based on solid evidence. So if we're having this conversation, there must be good reason—good basis—mustn't there?"

"Well...yes. I suppose." Doctor Fay Bones fiddled with his bland and stained tie.

"Then say it," said Sister Quiteria.

"Well...this is retrospect, mind you. And I haven't done any tests...but it did occur to me that possibly...well, Mother Rosalinda's symptoms are very similar to someone with radiation poisoning."

Sister Quiteria stopped walking and looked and Doctor Fay Bones.

"Now I know what you're going say. She's undergoing chemotherapy, so that's to be expected...and it is, but the nausea, vomiting, and diarrhea seem to have started earlier. Normally, in a cancer patient, they have some symptoms of cancer that are fairly benign-looking but persistent and annoying, and then after tests, you discover something deeper wrong," said Doctor Fay Bones, glad to get this off his chest. "You send them for the treatment and the treatment makes them in the short term much more ill, of course, because it's basically being poisoned, but...when I asked Mother Rosalinda, she said she'd had symptoms like that for a long time...almost since the start. It's only a theory, mind you. None of this means anything in itself, but I've started to wonder if her illness isn't just internal, so to speak, but...due to something in her environment and not...just pure chance. Of course, it probably is just pure chance. As I say...at this stage, it's only a theory."

"Don't apologise, Doctor Fay Bones," said Sister Quiteria. "However outlandish it sounds, for you to say it...it must be a serious suspicion, mustn't it?"

"Yes," said Doctor Fay Bones. "Only I took a look at her bone marrow and..."

By this time, they had reached the silage barn and stepped inside.

"Sorry, I must just sort something out with the silage. Will you wait here a moment?" said Sister Quiteria.

"Yes, certainly," said Doctor Fay Bones, rather confused.

Sister Quiteria went back on herself a moment, leaving Doctor Fay Bones standing inside the barn waiting for her.

—⁌⁍—

There was a strange smell in the barn. Doctor Fay Bones waited a while, feeling a bit uncomfortable. Next there was the sound of a wooden door slamming shut on him. Then it hit him. He was in the silage barn.

He started to cough. He spotted the yellowish-brown vapour, but he already knew it was there. He tried to run to the door...but he couldn't really run, so he walked. Then he crawled there. He felt very lightheaded. He coughed some more. He banged on the door.

He knew what would happen. Very soon his lungs would start to fill with fluid. He fell to his knees. He was feeling very weak. He felt his throat, eyes, and face burning as his saliva turned to nitric acid. He knew nitrogen oxide was heavier than air so he considered climbing higher, but there was nothing to climb on. Even if there had been, he didn't feel he had the strength in him. He felt the darkness creeping in. His face and throat felt like fire. It occurred to him that the door had been bolted. Then the darkness overwhelmed him.

Outside the barn, Sister Quiteria sat under a nearby tree, smiling, brooding, and calculating. She could smell the nitrogen dioxide, but kept her distance. She hurried to the door and undid the bolt, rubbed away her fingerprints with a handkerchief, then hurried away again downwind. The door slowly swung open. Doctor Fay Bones was dead, and if he wasn't, would be soon. Even if they revived him, he would die from the fluid downing his lungs before he said anything. Or he would have permanent brain damage. No one had seen them walk toward the barn. It was wet and starting to spit. Sister Quiteria's footprints in the mud would wash away soon. All she needed was to think up a plausible reason for why he might have gone in on his own. It was a piece of cake.

Chapter Fourteen

It was Sister Maria who found the body. In detective fiction, there were usually clues as to the fact someone met with an end that was calculated rather than an accident, and these could eventually be ascertained from the way they died. In reality, this did not always happen. There were no clues as to the fact that Doctor Fay Bones' death had been violent, because it had not been. The fact that it seemed a coincidence to have two accidental deaths on a farm at the same time, of course, did bother the Criminal Investigation Department, which did not believe in coincidence particularly in isolated rural areas. Probably because if they did believe in it, they would be out of work. However, in the real world, just because the police became bothered, it did not mean they would solve a case or even be able to prove there was one.

Detective Inspector Vale's investigation hit several snags. The first was that the nuns individually seemed to spend a lot of time alone, so asking them if they had an alibi seemed to reveal that there were about seven individuals who had the opportunity to do it if something had been done. Who had the motivation to do it was another question, which again seemed to yield no answer. Sister Maria seemed adamant that it was not an accident. "How can this be an accident?" she said. "He's a doctor. He would know not to go near the silage barn."

"Did he know that the barn was the silage barn?" said Detective Inspector Vale as they sat together in the refectory hall of the convent going over her statement. "It is a common form of death. There's been roughly one farm fatality every four months in our region for the past eighteen months according to Detective Constable Bland's research. Not that we've researched it much so far, but... I think you have to face facts...farm accidents do happen."

"I know," said Sister Maria. "But this is different. That is...it's like Sister Margaret's death...so unlikely."

"You were close to Sister Margaret?" asked Detective Inspector Vale.

"We were all close to her," said Sister Maria.

"And that's as far as it went?"

"Yes."

"I'm sorry," said Detective Inspector Vale. "It's just I have to ask these questions. However inappropriate it may seem."

"It does seem very inappropriate," interjected Father Baines who had found his way over to the table. Father Baines was the person Sister Maria had first broken the news to and it seemed to Detective Inspector Vale that he seemed to be hanging around her and them unnecessarily closely. He'd taken Sister Maria into the refectory for a bit of privacy. He hadn't expected Father Baines to follow so closely...making offers to make cups of tea and generally getting under his feet. At the same time, he didn't like to tell him to just go away. Funny, he didn't usually have a problem telling people to go away. Perhaps it was because he was a priest. That seemed a strange reason, though.

"Well," said Detective Inspector Vale, "we have read your book, Sister Maria."

"You have?" said Sister Maria.

"Yes, it's very unusual."

"The CDF thought so," interjected Father Baines.

Detective Inspector Vale gave Baines a cold look as if to say "*Now is not the time*," but he seemed to be impervious to cold looks...and quite a lot else besides...although he didn't show his disapprobation with hard stares or sarcastic tones. It was deeper than that, more complicated. He was difficult to read and Detective Inspector Vale flattered himself that he was good at reading people.

"You speak Italian?" asked Sister Maria.

"No," replied Detective Inspector Vale, "but we were able to get hold of an English translation."

"You must have been lucky. They've mostly been pulped now," said Sister Maria. "But they couldn't pulp the Italian version. Not legally."

"It's not really luck. If something may be relevant to a potential murder investigation, then we look into it...you understand. There's a lot in the book about lesbianism in the New Testament."

"I'm not a lesbian, if that's what you're trying to ask, Detective Inspector Vale," said Sister Maria. "The book does discuss the controversy around Romans 1:26, but you wouldn't expect a book on feminism in the church to avoid this subject. I am making a point that this passage hasn't always been used exclusively to condemn homosexuality. Clement of Alexandria thought it meant exclusively anal sex in the sense of penetrative..."

"I don't think we need to go..."—Detective Inspector Vale just managed to check himself before saying *"that deep"*—"into too much detail with regard to the theology. I was just asking some general questions."

"The thing is," said Sister Maria, "why would Doctor Fay Bones want to go for a walk round the convent when Father Baines here was waiting to drive him back to his surgery?"

"He doesn't have his own car?" asked Detective Inspector Vale.

"Yes, but he was in the area doing his rounds on his bicycle and when we called, he said he'd drop in as he was nearby. Actually, he often pops...popped by. He's religious himself," said Father Baines. "Says it keeps him fit...cycling that is, not praying...so I said...as we were taking up a lot of his time...or Mother Rosalinda was taking up a lot of it..."

"Where's his bike?" asked Detective Inspector Vale.

"It's in the boot of my car," said Father Baines. "It's one of those ones you can sort of fold up into a sort of metal cube."

"Show Bland," said Detective Inspector Vale.

Father Baines led Detective Constable Bland out to his car. "Wasn't it a bit odd for him to ask you to fold up his bike before he was leaving and put it in your boot?" said Detective Constable Bland.

"I don't follow," said Father Baines.

"Well," said Detective Constable Bland, "normally someone wouldn't put a bike...or anything else in the back of a car until just before they were actually leaving."

"Well, we didn't know when he was leaving exactly and neither did he," said Father Baines.

"That's exactly my point, sir," said Detective Constable Bland. "It's not a very coherent story."

"Sister Quiteria said it would be a good idea. You know, save time," said Father Baines, opening the boot, "if..."

"I see," said Detective Constable Bland, breaking off his flow. "So that's his bike, is it?"

"Yes," said Father Baines, "and that's his bag."

"And what's that?"

"I don't know," said Father Baines. He went to lift the item up.

"Don't touch any of it," said Detective Constable Bland, grabbing his hand tightly. "We need to check it for prints and forensics, you understand."

"No...oh...er...yes," said Father Baines.

Detective Constable Bland asked him if he would accompany himself and Detective Inspector Vale to the station.

Chapter Fifteen

Father Baines had been in a police station before. It was during what politicians now quaintly refer to as "the troubles." Father Baines hadn't caused any trouble during the troubles—not to his own recollection anyway—but the Royal Ulster Constabulary had rounded him up with the usual suspects...so he knew the drill. He wasn't shocked to find himself in a cell.

He realised that, in the end, sorting out these situations was usually simply a matter of stoically sitting and waiting and answering a lot of boring questions while someone stupid shouted. If the questions became more aggressive, he remembered he could ask if he could talk to a solicitor. Then usually they became less aggressive again, and eventually they would have to let him go if there was nothing to go on...which there wasn't.

He was not too worried. After all, one of the very few advantages of wearing a dog collar was that people tended to assume that you hadn't committed a crime. If the Anglican Bishop of Southwark could explain away being found drunk in the back of someone's car throwing children's toys about with the aside, "I'm the Bishop of Southwark, it's what I do," then surely Father Baines could explain away having a gas mask in the boot of his car with a dead man's DNA and his own fingerprints on. The trouble was, he found he couldn't.

"How do you explain having a gas mask in the boot of the car?" Detective Inspector Vale asked for the thirteenth time in the functional interview room.

"I don't know," said Father Baines. It was true; he didn't know. They sat silently again. Father Baines made a visual survey of the room for something to do. He liked the floor tiles. They were a nice dark blue, but he didn't think the pine table was an appropriate fit with the rest of the interior décor. "Why would I show you inside there if I knew it was there?"

"Because Sister Maria told us the bike was there, and I asked you to show it to us," said Detective Inspector Vale. "Or perhaps you'd forgotten it was there."

There was more silence. It was true he'd had no choice but to open the boot.

"Do you expect us to believe you just took the bike, put it in the boot of your car, and then went back in the convent just to wait for Doctor Fay Bones to stop talking to Sister Quiteria...which he already had, having gone out the back entrance by now? But you didn't know this," said Detective Inspector Vale. "Then sometime after that, someone got your car boot open without your car keys or your knowledge and planted that gas mask in there without either you or anyone else noticing...and in that time, about forty-five minutes before Sister Maria stumbled on Doctor Fay Bones' body, neither of you thought to ask the other where Doctor Fay Bones had gone?"

"I still thought he was with Mother Rosalinda and Sister Quiteria."

"And they still thought he was with you?"

"Yes."

"Doesn't seem very plausible," said Detective Inspector Vale, rubbing his chin. "I've been in this game quite a time, Father, and...well, you don't have to be Poirot to realise one of you two must be lying."

"What about Sister Maria?" suggested Father Baines. He didn't trust Sister Maria an inch.

"What about her?" replied Detective Inspector Vale. "You think she gassed him then waited forty-five minutes to come back to the house?"

"It could be an accident," said Father Baines.

"If it's an accident, wouldn't there be like a simple explanation for what a gas mask with your fingerprints on it was doing in the back of your car?"

"I don't know how my fingerprints got there," said Father Baines, for although he knew somewhere in the back of his mind that he had bought it with a load of other junk for the nuns' "museum/shop," he couldn't actually remember the when or where about that at this particular moment.

"Don't know much at all, do you?" said Detective Inspector Vale.

"No," said Father Baines, not realising Detective Inspector Vale would take this as sarcasm.

Detective Inspector Vale put his hands behind his head a moment and sat there pondering on Father Baines. "I notice you've got some form," he said eventually. "A caution for ass—"

"That was over ten years ago," snapped Father Baines.

"It may have been," said Detective Constable Bland, examining the folder himself, "but I'm afraid it stays on your file, Father, as a criminal record. And it shows a propensity to violence."

"Surely it should have expired by now?" said Father Baines, perspiring.

"In a year or a hundred," said Detective Constable Bland.

Detective Inspector Vale gave Detective Constable Bland a look.

Father Baines was about to say "*I want to talk to my solicitor*" when it occurred to him that perhaps his Bishop might be the better option. "I'm entitled to one phone call, aren't I?"

"Do not enough nuns know you're here already?" said Detective Inspector Vale.

"I want to talk to Bishop O'Flarty."

"Why?" said Detective Inspector Vale. "What's he going to do for you?"

"Pray," answered Father Baines. "You're barking up the wrong tree. You know there's going to be a big conference there tomorrow, and you know who's going, don't you? You do know about Imam Bakir coming over? You have looked into what's going on with Mr. Simbold and what the—"

"Father," said Detective Inspector Vale, "we're not picking on you. It's not one of your conspiracies. Yes, we do all know about your ranting on the Internet and having to be told to shut up by the powers that be in the RCC, but really...we're just doing our job. And our job is to follow the strongest leads. Now look at it from my point of view. After the death of Sister Margaret, I put everyone's photographs and details through the computer—mainly to get Edmund Ward off my back—and yours is the only one that came back with a record...and a record for violent crime. Okay, it was a caution, but people were let off things for political reasons if they played their cards right back then...and if they grassed on the right people."

"If I'd have '*grassed*' on people, I'd be six feet under," said Father Baines.

"Is that so?" said Detective Inspector Vale, becoming interested.

"You know what I mean. I didn't know anything much, but people all knew—"

"Yes, I do know, Father," said Detective Inspector Vale, "but that's exactly the kind of statement we can use in evidence against you. The fact remains that you still have form. You still have a conviction for a violent crime—and a caution is a conviction. People don't sign them unless they have no choice."

"That's not what you said at the time."

"It wasn't me that made you sign it. I wasn't there at the time, and you have a gas mask with your fingerprints on it in the boot of your car next to the bike of a gassed man. You were the person who found the body of Sister Margaret too, weren't you? Coincidence? If you were me, who would you start with as your number one suspect?"

"I want to talk to Bishop O'Flarty," said Father Baines.

Chapter Sixteen

"The problem is," said Mother Rosalinda, "that my dealer wants me to go. He said we should bring it forward because if we wait till when the retrospective is supposed to start, then...well, not wishing to depress any of you...I might not be here. Doctor Fay Bones—God rest him—was very clear. I don't have long to live. And apparently moving the date allows myself and the Palin Brothers to exhibit in the same place...under the same banner...which would be an artistic first."

"The trouble is it clashes with the ecumenical conference, which we...you've...we've all spent such a long time putting together," said Sister Maria.

"I know," said Mother Rosalinda. "I know I must tell them I can't go. It's not that important that I'm there rather than here, is it? I mean...that is to say...that here is where I belong, isn't it? But I thought I'd tell you. For some reason, every decision seems so much harder when you have little or no time."

"No, you must go," said Sister Quiteria. Then reading the temperature in the room, she clarified this. "That is...I think perhaps you should go if you want to. I wouldn't say you shouldn't go. The ecumenical conference is a week, so you'll still be here for most of it. You'd only really be away for one day, maybe half of the next day."

Mother Rosalinda eased back in her chair and closed her eyes a moment. "I know and that's very kind of you to say that, but it still feels wrong," she said. "I'd feel like I was abandoning you for one thing...particularly with everything else that's been going on. After all, it may only be a matter of time before the police charge Father Baines...from what I hear, and then the place could rapidly turn into another..."

"Media circus?" said Sister Quiteria.

"Edmund Ward is already having a field day running us down to any newspaper that will listen for managing to have two farm accidents so close together...and a number of people have cancelled their stays...even Mr. Simbold has said he's not sure he can host events here. Mind you, I had already said to him that I was beginning to wonder how appropriate it was for us to associate with a political organisation so closely because there will always be people who say—"

"I think perhaps you should go too," interjected Sister Maria. "That is to say..." She looked around at the other nuns to ascertain if she had their support. No one seemed negative to the idea. Not even the older nuns. "There are many forms of ecumenism, aren't there? Perhaps having your work next to the Palin Brothers and their mockery of religious iconography will cause people to...well..."

"Laugh?" interjected Sister Luciana. "I don't think you need to share a platform with people like that, Mother Rosalinda. They are revolting men who create revolting art and...well, you know what they did to one of your paintings...sickening. Blasphemy. Ignorant bullies. Look at the people who collect them. That wife beater man and his brother...nasty pieces of work. That's who they sell to."

There was an awkward silence. Sister Luciana never said much really.

"Jesus was laughed at," said Sister Quiteria weakly. "We mustn't be afraid to enter the public square simply because we might be mocked for our beliefs."

"That is very true," said Mother Rosalinda. "Fortunately, there is no great rush to make an immediate permanent decision about whether I am going or not...but I think I will certainly tell them that I agree to the earlier date. I may find when it comes that I am not well enough to go anyway, and the problem will then be solved by Our Lord. It is he who should decide in the end. All we can do is consider what he would best want for us. Certainly the gallery may have a point that in terms of publicising the exhibition, it would help their commercial venture if I was still alive at least at the start of it."

"As I remember," said Sister Maria, "before he...went to his eternal reward, Doctor Fay Bones said that actually... although the prognosis is 'bleak,' I think the word he used...you may still have a prolonged remission even if you don't..."

"Recover?" said Mother Rosalinda. "Sister Maria, I have told you before you must not be shy to discuss such things. I have kept no secrets from you and have been open with you all, for we are all Sisters of Christ here. We are all servants of Him, and we have dedicated our lives to Him. We should not be afraid to finally meet Our Lord. That is in the end where all our journeys take us. Some of our journeys will take us there faster than others. That is all. We must make the best of every day and every hour that is given to us. That is what He would want. I realise when I have gone it will be upsetting for some of you, but I say to you...we must all put our faith in Christ. None of us really know what tomorrow will bring. As Matthew says, Our Lord says to his disciples in Chapter 24 verse 42 'Therefore, stay awake, for you do not know on what day your Lord is coming. But know this, that if the master of the house had known in what part of the night the thief was coming, he would have stayed awake and would not have let his house be broken into. Therefore you also must be ready, for the Son of Man is coming at an hour you do not expect'."

Sister Quiteria smiled.

Chapter Seventeen

Bishop O'Flarty demanded to see Detective Inspector Vail. The policeman on reception was not very helpful, but there were times when being a bishop was an advantage. Keeping a bishop waiting was not the same as keeping Joe or Jane Bloggs waiting. Dog collars were conspicuous in any waiting room. It was their function.

However, Detective Inspector Vale was very good at being single-minded and ignoring people when he wanted to. He had Father Baines on the run, or rather he had Father Baines in an interview room unable to run away from the fact he had no alibi, no explanation, and no way out.

The clock was ticking and he'd have to either charge Baines or let him go very soon. The last thing he needed was Detective Constable Bland bothering him about some Bishop...or Chief Inspector Hawkins bothering Detective Constable Bland about some bishop. Detective Inspector Vale didn't have a big thing against bishops. He wasn't a militant atheist, but they made him uneasy. All those religious people made him uneasy. He suspected the only reason Superintendent Hawkins and Detective Constable Bland were bothering him was that they too were too uneasy for similarly irrational reasons.

"This is stupid," said Detective Inspector Vale for what seemed like the millionth time. "We've got DNA. You can't offer us any rational or logical explanation of why the gas mask was in your car. You're going to have to do better than this."

"I didn't do it," said Father Baines, rather calmly considering the amount of time he'd been there and the number of different ways there were of saying that you haven't done something.

"And you're not going to give us anything more than that?" said Detective Inspector Vale.

"What, exactly, am I supposed to give you?" said Father Baines.

"An explanation, Father. Or I'm going to have to charge you. You know that, don't you?"

"That's up to you," said Father Baines.

Detective Inspector Vale didn't get it. The man seemed to just not care what happened to him. "You're taking this very calmly," he said, sitting back in his chair and looking at the knotholes in the fake pine table top. "Are you trying to tell me you did do it?"

"I'm not trying to tell you anything," said Father Baines.

"You're trying not to tell me something?" said Detective Inspector Vale.

"I'm not not trying to tell you anything either," said Father Baines. "That is...I've told you what I do know...and that should be enough. If you want to know more than that and I don't know it...there isn't very much I can do about that, is there? If you ask me, this is persecution. I think you hate religion, Detective Inspector Vale, and I represent it, so..."

Detective Inspector Vale laughed a hollow laugh and chewed the end of his biro. The plastic cracked a little. He heard it and felt a small piece of plastic on his tongue. He put the biro down. He fished out the little bit of plastic. He threw it in the bin.

"I think this is persecution," repeated Father Baines. "I think your real problem is that I'm a priest."

"Why would that be a problem?"

"Did you really need to be snooping around the convent as much as you were after Sister Margaret died?" said Father Baines. "For such a long time? I think you're just overly suspicious of us because of what we do. It's clear what happened. For some reason, the doctor went into the barn and was overcome by the fumes."

"I don't believe in coincidences."

"You have a very suspicious mind, Detective Inspector, and I know it is your job," said Father Baines, "but maybe it isn't healthy. You know the church has always suffered from persecution?"

"I don't think my mind's as suspicious as yours," said Detective Inspector Vale. "Did you think being a priest put you beyond suspicion?"

"No."

There was a knock at the door.

"Come in," said Detective Inspector Vale.

It was Detective Constable Bland. He looked apologetic.

"Well, Bland?"

"I think you should see the bishop, sir," said Detective Constable Bland.

"Should I?"

"He has some information."

"Does he?"

"I do," said a voice. It was Bishop O'Flarty. He didn't ask if he could enter the interview room. He walked through the gap between Detective Constable Bland and the pine doorframe, and the detective constable didn't try to stop him. He had come in full vestments, so he sort of glided in. He stopped a foot and a half from Detective Inspector Vale. "Please let this man go. He has done nothing criminal. As you can see," said Bishop O'Flarty. He was holding out some paper.

"What's this?" said Detective Inspector Vale, annoyed.

"It's a print out from an Internet forum," said Bishop O'Flarty.

"As you can see from the dates and times of the posts," chipped in Detective Constable Bland, "Father Baines couldn't have been anywhere near Doctor Fay Bones at the time of his death. He was—"

"Online," said Bishop O'Flarty menacingly. "Where he's not allowed to be. Oh, yes, I know you go on there, Baines. When I said stop blogging, I meant stop posting anywhere on the Internet until I tell you otherwise. Not make up handles that everyone knows are you because your prose style is identical right down to the spelling mistakes. Of course I can't prove it is him completely, but I'm pretty sure you'll find that the email address and the site account connect together."

"It was me, My Lord Bishop," said Father Baines.

"You see," said Bishop O'Flarty, "Baines here is a bit of a p...spiritual worry to me as I don't think he's been responding to our critics with...charity and love...and so I've told him not to talk in public for a while...while he cogitates on his spiritual relationship with his brothers and sisters in Christ. But, obviously, I still keep an eye on him, and so I just thought that I would check some of the sites on the Internet where he frequently...that he frequents...and I found he was on the Internet at the supposed time of Doctor Fay Bones' death. He was busy being rude to people, his favourite pastime."

"All a bit convenient," said Detective Inspector Vale.

"It's true," said the bishop. "I asked Mother Rosalinda to check the nuns' computer, which they hardly ever use, and it seems he'd been using it. The browser records someone was on these pages. So I asked her to print it out. I mean...who else could it be?"

"So why was there a gas mask in the boot of his car?" asked Detective Inspector Vale.

"I don't know. You're the detective," said the bishop.

"Yes, I am, aren't I?"

"I'm sorry if you've been barking up the wrong tree," said Bishop O'Flarty with fake pity to piss him off.

It did.

Chapter Eighteen

Just when Detective Inspector Vale thought he could not suffer any more social humiliation, Chief Inspector Hawkins appeared at the door.

"Ah, Vale," he said. The Chief Inspector was a mercurial character who never seemed to appear in places like interview rooms if he could help it and had a Cheshire Cat-like ability to dematerialise with an avuncular smile in difficult political situations. He was one of those old-fashioned policemen who said they believed in hands-on policing and yet always seem to be too subsumed with paperwork and dealing with minor political functionaries and committees to do any actual policing.

As far as Detective Inspector Vale was concerned, the function of the Chief Inspector was to keep politicians, do-gooders, and the press out of his remaining strands of hair so he could get on with what was his real vocation—nicking villains—unimpeded by well-meaning idiots who spend their time reading the Guardian or watching Panorama on BBC1.

"Do you have a moment?"

It was of course a rhetorical question. The Chief Inspector did not actually care whether Detective Inspector Vale actually had a moment. He was telling him to make time.

"DC Bland can you take over?" said Detective Inspector Vale, happy to extricate himself from the withering stares of Bishop O'Flarty, which were all the more harrowing to him because they seemed to everyone else to be benign.

The Chief Inspector didn't ask Detective Inspector Vale to follow him to his office. Detective Inspector Vale just followed him out of habit. He knew what to expect. A bollocking on the subject of not locking up innocent members of the clergy cloaked in sarcastic passive aggression. He was wrong.

In the room was a man. A portly sixty-year-old man—if that was still old these days. He had a slightly schoolboy quality to his haggard face. He wore a brown suit and a grey v-neck jumper.

Detective Inspector Vale considered how odd it was for anyone to wear a brown suit these days. He never heard a description, "IC1 Male Dark Hair Blue Eyes Brown Suit," but here one was.

"Hello," said the man in a voice that seemed to say, *I've been to a very good boarding school, but I never mention it.* "I'm Sir Frederick Didcot from SIS. Take a seat." He didn't wait for the Chief Inspector to introduce him and the Chief Inspector didn't seem bothered by not being introduced, which was unusual.

"I'll leave you two alone," said Chief Inspector Hawkins, simply and diplomatically. He closed the door, shutting himself outside his own office and Detective Inspector Vale inside.

Detective Inspector Vale took a seat.

Sir Frederick Didcot smiled smile as if to say, *It's okay, you're not in trouble or anything.* "The Chief Inspector told me about your...investigation into the convent. It's not going very well, is it?" He came straight to the point.

"No," said Detective Inspector Vale without questioning what business it was of Sir Frederick Didcot's, "it isn't."

"Difficult, arresting any member of the clergy," said Sir Frederick. "Even in this day and age when there are so many of them in prison for...erm...things."

"Yes."

"You're on the right lines, though. These have to be inside jobs. Obviously, there is something wrong at that convent—even a fool would realise that there has to be. You don't have to be Miss Marple to figure that out, but...well...the reason I'm here is, to cut to the chase, as the Americans say...your Detective Constable...Band?"

"Bland," corrected Detective Inspector Vale helpfully.

"Yes, well, anyway, you asked him to do some facial recognitions on your computer some time ago...on all the nuns...and suspects?"

"Yes."

"And you didn't pick up anything."

"No, we just ran it through the database."

"Yes," said Sir Frederick awkwardly. "What I'm going to tell you now, Detective Inspector Vale, is classified. So that means it goes no farther than this room. You understand?"

"Yes," said Detective Inspector Vale, trying to look serious.

"When you run a face through the police computer...if certain criteria are met...if it's a person that we have interest in, then that gets picked up by GCHQ and forwarded on back to our HQ at SIS."

"I don't think that's exactly a big secret," said Detective Inspector Vale. "I kind of guessed as much."

"Yes, well, don't take out advertising on it even if it is a small secret," said Sir Frederick. "Remember big secrets are usually just small secrets joined together." He passed a file over the desk. It was an old-fashioned looking file.

Detective Inspector Vale had sort of expected to receive something digital or more modern looking. "One of your agents?" he asked after opening it.

"Ex-agents," replied Sir Frederick. "She's on the run, so to speak. To use the popular terminology, she's 'gone rogue.'"

"You want us to run her in?"

"Er...no...I mean...of course I'd like very much to 'run her in,' but it's not that simple."

"I thought it wasn't."

"She has something we want."

"I thought she might."

"The thing is, we've actually known where she is for quite a while, but...well...there's no point in doing anything if she's not a threat, is there? Also, she has something we want, and we don't want it to fall into the wrong hands."

"I don't suppose you can tell us what that is?" asked Detective Inspector Vale with a sigh.

"It's classified," said Sir Frederick.

"I thought it might be," said Detective Inspector Vale.

"Look, Vale," said Sir Frederick. "We might want you to run her in, but not yet. I don't know if you know, but the nuns are hosting an ecumenical conference. It starts tomorrow. We believe that Sister Quiteria—as you know her—will be meeting someone there. I mean, she'll be meeting and greeting lots of people, obviously, but she's also going to meet someone in particular. Someone she's going to pass this object onto...for cash." He showed Detective Inspector Vale another photo. "We will 'bring her in,' but I need to select the right moment."

"What is it?" asked Detective Inspector Vale. It just looked in the photo like a length of steel.

Sir Frederick looked at him awkwardly.

"I see...it's so important you won't tell me about it? You may as well tell me. I'll probably see it when you find it."

"It's a Uranium fuel rod."

"You what?"

"Well, you did ask."

"How did you lose a Uranium fuel rod?"

"I'm not sure really, but a number of them did go missing in the 1950s when Windscale caught fire. We've been trying to recover them since, obviously, but it's not the sort of thing you can take out publicity on."

"I can imagine," said Detective Inspector Vale.

"It's not like losing a cat."

"No."

"Have you heard of an Imam Bakir?"

Chapter Nineteen

The Eccumenical Conference came and so did the representatives of religions the world over. Priests, Vicars, Rabbis, Imams, Bishops, Deacons, Sanghas, Brahmans... It was, as always, quite an occasion, and although she wasn't there, Mother Rosalinda at least had the comfort of knowing Sister Quiteria's careful management would make sure it would be a success...at least in financial and logistical terms.

Her faith was not misplaced. Sister Maria knew in which rooms each of the delegates were staying and what special diets they required, and the liaison with the outside caterers was faultless. This was more than could be said of previous years. No one was quite sure what the Buddhist contingent were doing there, but somehow Sister Quiteria managed to get the Dalai Lama in person rather than his representative to come along, which was a bit of a publicity coup for the convent. Mr. Simbold attended too, of course, in a personal capacity and not on behalf of United Kingdom Independence Party, although he had never been formally invited and seemed somehow to end up helping with the administration. Sister Quiteria insisted he was needed to help her with the logistics when questioned by Sister Luciana, and no one seemed to argue with her much anymore. Not even Sister Luciana.

Exactly what they were discussing at the conference was of little or no interest to Sister Quiteria, who saw herself simply as Head of Administration in the absence of Mother Rosalinda. It was probably all some exercise in sorting out territorial disputes and inter-denominational turf wars to her mind.

Sister Quiteria didn't think much of or about theology.

She was only really interested in one other person at the conference. It was, of course, Imam Bakir. At the welcoming party (it wasn't much of a party in her view, but she still felt she had to keep up appearances by not doing anything too exciting), she found the space and time to take him out into the gardens.

"Good of you to come, Imam Bakir," she said.

"Is this really necessary?" he asked. "I understand you have to have a cover of some kind, but surely hiding out in a convent is taking things a bit far?"

"You got into the country without too many questions, didn't you?" replied Sister Quiteria. "The old rouses are the best, Mr. Bakir. I will admit it is something of a cliché in terms of history and literature, but clichés are clichés because they work. I've managed quite successfully, you must admit, to keep off SIS's radar."

"You're sure of that? Or do they actually know you're here and turn a blind eye? Or are they waiting for something to happen?"

"Does it matter?"

"Yes, because if it's the latter, I may have walked into a trap and so might you."

"We haven't," said Sister Quiteria confidently.

"And the rod?"

"I have it."

"It's here?"

Sister Quiteria smiled a *Come off it, I'm not that stupid smile*. "It's not far from here. I can get my hands on it...when you get the money transfer sorted."

"We'll be doing it tomorrow when I've seen the merchandise. Where is it?"

"You'll see it before you part with the money."

"Good," said Mr. Bakir. "Sister Maria tells me that the Mother Superior has been taken down with some form of cancer."

"Yes," said Sister Quiteria. "Very sad."

"Radiation sickness?" queried Mr. Bakir.

"It might have been," said Sister Quiteria impassively.

"That explains why her doctor had to die then. We have been busy, haven't we? What about the nun who was killed by her own tractor?"

"Purely an accident."

"Your neighbours don't seem to think so, nor do the papers. Are you sure you're not under any observation? This all sounds very flakey to me."

"Plod round here are incredibly stupid."

"Plod?"

"English vernacular for the police."

—⁓⁓—

At this moment, someone hailed them. It was a Rabbi—or at least it was dressed like one, and had claimed to be one to Sister Maria. He was elderly. He was smiling. "Hello," he said, "I'm sorry to bother you, but you're both under arrest." He pulled out a Glock 17 pistol. "I'd prefer it if you came quietly."

"Does it matter if we don't?" asked Mr. Bakir.

"No, but I'd prefer it," said the man.

"I'm sure you would, Sir Frederick," replied Sister Quiteria. "But you won't get the rod either if we don't discuss terms, will you?"

"I know it's got to be on the estate somewhere," said Sir Frederick. "We'll find it—all it takes is a Geiger counter."

"Is that how you lost it for nearly five decades in the first place?" asked Sister Quiteria. "Honestly, do you really think I'd be so stupid as to keep it stored here?"

"Yes," said Sir Frederick. "I do. We've had you both under observation for quite a while...or at least Detective Inspector Vale has without being bright enough to know I was reading his reports. You can fool some of the police inspectors some of the time, but you can't fool SIS at all."

"You don't sound sure," said Sister Quiteria.

Sir Frederick Didcot smiled as benignly as he could with a Glock 17 in his hand. "Don't play games. The game is up. Please just show me."

"Very well. Follow me," said Sister Quiteria, and headed off toward the chapel. Mr. Bakir followed. Sir Didcot followed Bakir.

Sister Quiteria went inside first. They followed her. The doorway was wide. No obvious danger. Sir Didcot suspected it was a trap, but he had his alarm on him in case he needed backup. He was aware he was entering enemy territory, but he had the gun too. What could go wrong? They didn't have guns...or at least he thought they were unarmed, but why should they be? Then again, why shouldn't they be?

In case they were armed, he told them to keep their hands up and keep their distance, even though it always sounded corny and he felt he shouldn't have to say it at all. He wasn't going to let them get close enough to try a disarm procedure. He really wanted to separate them from the rest of the group so they could be arrested without too much attention if possible. The place had too much attention already. If they led him to the rod without too much bother, that was so much for the better. He had them at a safe distance, but not too far away...and then it happened.

Although he had thought he had them alone, someone else had been there. It was Edmund Ward. He'd actually come to deliver a letter from his solicitor to Mother Rosalinda about the death of his sister. He'd entered unseen behind Sir Frederick Didcot.

Sensing something, Sir Frederick turned.

It was all the distraction Sister Quiteria needed. The moment Sir Frederick Didcot swivelled round to check who was behind him, she vaulted forward and disarmed him, using classic military intelligence moves.

The gun clattered away under a confessional box where no one could reach it. Sir Frederick was lithe, but he was still a sexagenarian.

Edmund ran forward, but Mr. Bakir hit him hard on the back of the head with a handy statue of St. Anthony of Padua, chipping it slightly.

Sir Didcot and Sister Quiteria battled on while Bakir attempted to recover the Glock from under the confessional. By the time Bakir realised he could not get it out, Sister Quiteria was busy drowning Sir Frederick in the font.

Sir Frederick wouldn't say the whole of his life rushed before his eyes, as obviously he'd been a field agent himself in his youth and knew what to expect, but he had visions of several internal reports he had yet to complete. He reached for his alarm, but she prevented him with one hand while with the other held his head under.

—⊷⟳⊶—

It seemed to take a long time, but eventually Didcot stopped moving.

"That was close," said Bakir.

"Yes," said Sister Quiteria, pulling the personal alarm from Didcot's pocket and lowering him gently to the floor.

"Where can we hide the bodies?"

"One of the wonderful things about churches is that they usually have a crypt specifically for just that." Of course, the crypt wasn't actually specifically for just that, but they used it for that anyway.

Chapter Twenty

Why people actually needed to build crypts was beyond Sister Quiteria, but fortunately, as she pointed out, there was one, and it was dark, damp, and seldom used. It had been used regularly once, but not since before the reformation.

They dragged the bodies down there and hid them under some old furniture. Edmund was still alive, so Sister Quiteria made sure he was dead with her bare hands.

They went back upstairs and managed as best they could to clear the place up so it looked like nothing had happened there to the casual observer. Hopefully no one would notice the statue of St. Anthony of Padua was now missing the Christ child's head.

Just as they were about to leave, the door of the confessional swung open suddenly and out emerged Father Baines holding the Glock. He had obviously seen the whole thing.

Sister Quiteria wondered if he even knew how to use the gun, but as it was a fairly simple weapon, she thought they'd better not chance it.

"Stop," said Father Baines. "Yes, I saw what you did."

"But you didn't call for help?" said Sister Quiteria.

"No," replied Father Baines. "Sir Didcot was quite clear about the mission—to recover the rod first at all costs. Individual lives are not as important as that."

They both stared at him blankly.

Sir Didcot had not actually said exactly this when he asked for Father Baines' help—it was a bit of an extrapolation. Father Baines had seen the whole thing from inside the confessional. He had just been too scared to get involved until he had the gun. Even now he was scared.

"Yes, he recruited me." He smiled. "Interesting, isn't it? I said this conference was wrong, and I said there was something wrong going on here, but of course everyone thinks they know better, don't they? Traitors to the faith like Bishop O'Flarty don't think the church has to do anything to protect itself. They think Vatican II just made all our enemies go away. Well, I told them there was an enemy within, and I was right, wasn't I?"

"Yes," said Mr. Bakir, holding his hands up. "They were."

"Where's the rod?" said Father Baines, thinking it sounded odd.

"I'll take you to it," said Sister Quiteria.

"Well I wasn't going to trust you to just tell me where it is," said Father Baines, enjoying feeling like he was James Bond. He indicated toward the door with his gun. Fortunately, as it was a formal occasion, he had his full vestments on so it was fairly easy to conceal a gun beneath them.

As they got nearer to the main convent building, the Dalai Lama came out to congratulate Sister Quiteria on her organisation of the conference. It was deeply awkward.

"I'm glad I came," he said. "It is, as you promised, a really beautiful location for meditation."

"There is no need for temples, no need for complicated philosophy. Our own brain, our own heart is our temple; the philosophy is kindness," said Sister Quiteria.

"Very good," said the Dalai Lama. "All the same, you must be sad to be leaving."

"It is for the best," said Sister Quiteria.

"You will excuse me," said the Dalai Lama. "I have some details to go through with Mr. Simbold to do with the finances."

"Yes, of course," said Sister Quiteria.

He withdrew back into the house.

"What was all that about?" asked Father Baines, curious.

"Just paperwork to do with the conference," said Sister Quiteria.

"Keep moving," said Father Baines.

—◦⦿◦—

Sister Quiteria led Father Baines through a room of chatting people who they superficially acknowledged and then on into the cloister...and on from there to Mother Rosalinda's cell. It had a large oak door. She opened it using her own key.

Sister Quiteria had made certain she had keys for everything very soon after joining the order. Mother Rosalinda wasn't very bright. She kept a set of spare keys in a draw in her office. It was simply a matter of finding an excuse to go into the village and get another one cut. Although why nuns needed to lock their doors was another question.

"It was in here all along?" said Mr. Bakir.

"Of course," said Sister Quiteria, entering. "Safest place. Mother Rosalinda's far too holy to clean under her own bed."

"You realise you've been murdering her?" said Father Baines.

"I do. And I don't give a stuff," said Sister Quiteria, putting on a pair of surgical gloves she had on her person in order to handle the rod. "I'm beyond caring. It was necessary." She removed the rod from the underside of the bed where it was taped in place by masking tape. The tape was quite strong, and there was quite a lot of it, so she had to pull hard.

The rod was as Father Baines had expected it to be—a rod. Metal. About a metre long. Funny, it didn't look like much, but it obviously was. Enough Uranium 235 to make a very dirty bomb.

"I feel a bit sad that she's going to die, but then isn't this place a sort of living death anyway? Never going out. Never meeting anybody but the other nuns. It's as if someone took death and set it in aspic."

This kind of missed out the reality that actually Mother Rosalinda did go out, but even Father Baines had to admit there was some truth in it. They were living for the next life, not this one.

While Father Baines was cogitating on how insulting this description of religious life was, Sister Quiteria had him at close range. She wacked him suddenly round the head with the rod—very hard.

Although it was a small room, she had plenty of space to get momentum behind it. He didn't expect it. He tried to duck, but she got him good. Sister Quiteria managed to grab the gun first too as soon as he dropped it—much to the chagrin of Mr. Bakir.

"What do we do with the body?" asked Mr. Bakir.

"Under the bed," said Sister Quiteria. "Mother Rosalinda's not coming back until tomorrow. It'll be safe there until then. You do it."

Mr. Bakir didn't argue. He did it. "What do we do now?" he asked.

"Rejoin the conference," said Sister Quiteria.

"And the rod?"

"I'll leave it here," she said. "I'll lock it in. It'll be fine."

"How do you know I won't be able to pick the lock or something?"

"It doesn't matter if you can. You're going to be spending the night with me. In fact," she said, concealing the gun beneath her habit, "you're going to be with me all the time. You're never going out of my sight."

"What if someone's waiting for Didcot or Baines to sign in or something?"

"Well, you've got a tablet in your room. There's a good signal. The faster you can convince me you've made the cash transfer, the faster we can both get out of here, can't we?"

After Mr. Bakir checked the corridor was clear, they left the room.

She locked the door behind them. As she did, Sister Maria came running toward them. She stopped. She was panting.

Mr. Bakir looked as though he was going to attack her.

Sister Quiteria grabbed his arm to stop him, hoping Sister Maria hadn't noticed her doing it.

"Sister Quiteria!" exclaimed Sister Maria, looking very pale. No more words came out for a long time until she continued. "I've just had a call from the Palin brothers." It could only mean one thing. Mother Rosalinda was dead. She had died on the train up to London before she even got to the exhibition.

Chapter Twenty-One

"Go! Go! Go!" shouted Detective Inspector Vale as Mr. Simbold's car emerged from the convent. He and Detective Constable Bland ran from their unmarked Vauxhall Astra, weapons at the ready. The nearest thing the UK had to what the USA would call a SWAT team bundled out of another unmarked van.

Detective Inspector Vale liked this bit. *I love nicking villains*, he thought. Detective Constable Bland liked it too—it made him feel like he was in *Die Hard*. It was what he had joined the force for.

Unfortunately, there was a problem. At the same time, a large number of gay rights activists burst out of the pub over the road and started pelting Mr. Simbold's car with pots of coloured paint and eggs. Simultaneous to this, a couple of local reporters who had also been in the Harrow public house not purely by coincidence also rushed out and photographed the ensuing pandemonium. The protestors had heard someone shouting "Go! Go! Go!" but inaccurately assumed it was one of them spotting the car with Simbold in.

The protestors had been waiting for their chance to humiliate Mr. Simbold in a more inventive way than dumping manure outside the convent again for some time. They had waited for this moment . They were calculating that with the Dalai Lama being in the Convent at the same time as Mr. Simbold, a visual protest would get them not just in the papers, but gain them maximum publicity—hopefully the BBC News. Possibly even get them on the news. They knew both were in there. Several of the group were also Tamils who had a whole separate lot of grudges against Mr. Simbold.

As usual, it wasn't Mr. Simbold himself who was the primary source of the vituperation now directed at him. Much of it was down to the extremely thinly veiled homophobic comments his deputy Mr. McWilliams seemed to manage to make on twitter, which always seemed to end up attributed to him in the local paper somehow. These, in turn, had merged in the public mind with a large number of other unpopular and ill-informed comments Mr. McWilliams had also made on different issues to do with Sri Lankan politics. The two causes had become one. If the gays wanted a fight, the gay Tamils really wanted a fight, and they in turn had recruited straight Tamils.

Anyway, they had been waiting for most of the weekend for Mr. Simbold to come out of the convent. If not keeping a round the clock vigil at least keeping a round-the-pub-during-opening-hours vigil. Suddenly, this was their moment.

One can full of paint missed Mr. Simbold's car, completely drenching Detective Inspector Vale and Detective Constable Bland in paint and making them fall over. A second can achieved the obscuration of Mr. Simbold's car windscreen with paint while another missile cracked it.

Mr. Simbold felt that he should speed off as fast as possible, as this was obviously some kind of assassination attempt. But being unable to see properly, he simply sped into the back of the police van, severely wounding several officers in the process. Both vehicles were undriveable wrecks.

—⌛—

Detective Inspector Vale stood up, slipped on some paint, and fell over again.

"Homophobic fascist cunt!" someone shouted.

"Shit man—you've painted the Po Po!" shouted someone else. The activists scarpered. The press also scarpered...at least back to the pub where there was some cover.

Sister Quiteria was on the back seat of the car from where she could cover both Mr. Simbold, who was in the driving seat and Mr. Bakir who was in the front passenger seat with the Glock. She opened her door and made a run for it, closely followed by Mr. Bakir.

Mr. Bakir's side of the car, however, was the side where the paint was on the ground. He slipped on it and fell over.

Mr. Simbold, of course, didn't know what was going on. He'd just agreed to give them a lift to the station as Mr. Bakir had a phone call calling him away on urgent business shortly after Sister Quiteria told them that unfortunately she needed to go up to town to identify Mother Rosalinda.

Mother Rosalinda had been found dead in her seat when her train pulled into Victoria Station. If she hadn't had correspondence on her from the gallery, they wouldn't have known who she was.

Sister Quiteria was worried SIS had them under observation and had thought they looked less conspicuous with Simbold than driving in the vomit yellow Austin Allegro, which she'd made sure couldn't start by pulling off a spark plug wire.

Mr. Simbold had been a bit curious as to what Mr. Bakir was doing with a set of golf clubs (the answer was concealing that he was carrying about a Uranium fuel rod), but "Imam" Bakir's answer that "Muslims play golf too" had more than satisfied him as he was a man of little imagination. He hadn't even realised Sister Quiteria had a gun trained on him and "Imam" Bakir.

The wreck of Mr. Simbold's car and the police van blocked the main road in a southerly direction, so Sister Quiteria made her escape through the adjoining churchyard and over the fields.

Mr. Bakir couldn't run. His leg had been hurt, not badly, but it was bruised enough to stop him running. The collision had also significantly reduced the number of pursuing policemen to Detective Inspector Vale, Detective Constable Bland, and another armed officer carrying an automatic weapon. Most of the other policemen either had a broken limb, or were unconscious, mangled, or dead. It was dusk. The field of cauliflowers was wet and muddy, and in case the three pursuing officers or Sister Quiteria didn't feel as though they were under armed attack, the bird scaring machines were still going *Bang! Bang! Bang!* at regular intervals around them.

Sister Quiteria knew what she had to do. She turned. She had anticipated the actions of the authorised firearms officer.

He had also stopped and was taking aim with his semi-automatic carbine. She took aim at him with her Glock. He was the one she had to bring down. Vale and Bland had very little chance of hitting her from that range with their hand weapons. They might wing her if they were lucky, but they were not trained marksmen. The officer took aim slowly through his holographic sights.

Sister Quiteria was SIS trained to use a large number of weapons with deadly accuracy from a range of distances. She shot first. It was a direct hit to the brain. He was dead instantly. His bulletproof jacket was useless.

Vale and Bland stopped in their tracks.

She took aim on Bland. She could see him starting to move for cover, but he was too slow. She took him out too—bullet to the head. Lucky, she thought, but of course it wasn't luck. It was training.

—⚬⚭⚬—

Detective Inspector Vale hit the ground, throwing himself face-down in the dirt. When he looked up, Sister Quiteria was running again. He followed her at a distance and saw her jump over a stone wall at the far end of the field. Slowly, he approached it. He peeked over. Then he looked over fully.

On the other side of the small stone wall was the cliff path and beyond the cliff, nothing—just a sheer drop onto the rocks and sea below. He looked up and down the cliff path. She was not there. There was nowhere else to go. He looked down onto the rocks that the sea was lapping over. If she was down there, she was dead. He was more than slightly scared to be so near the edge. What if it were to give way? What if she were to run out and push him?

She didn't. He never saw her again. Neither did any other policeman or policewoman despite a massive search of the entire area using every method available including infra-red cameras and police helicopters. Sister Quiteria had gone.

Chapter Twenty-Two

Mother Rosalinda's funeral was an odd and doubly sad affair as it happened on the day the nuns were leaving for good. She was the last nun to be buried there. Father Baines was buried next to her.

The Palin Brothers couldn't make it, but sent a wreath in the shape of Mother Rosalinda sitting on a giant dildo even though the nuns had stated quite clearly that they only wanted charitable donations, not flowers.

Bishop O'Flarty had mixed emotions, being very upset by the death of Mother Rosalinda but quite glad that the Lord had chosen to take Father Baines back unto himself. If only the Lord took everyone who caused division and dissent unto himself, his life would be so much easier...but then he might not have anything to do.

Of course, the downside of this was he now had to deal with Mother Maria and her attempts to mix religion with feminism instead of mixing it with art like Mother Rosalinda had done. Annoying as Father Baines had been, his angry online antics had often prevented the bishop from having to argue with people personally. He could just send Father Baines somewhere and know that there would eventually be an argument that would keep a person out of his thinning hair. He didn't even have to ask Baines to start one. It was what he did.

At the convent, the Buddhist community was already there, as the nuns themselves had moved to a rather uninspiring converted office block in which they were trying to set up some kind of Government Free School.

Although the Dalai Lama Trust were very understanding of the fact that the nuns had obviously been the victims of a cruel financial property fraud, they still felt that they had parted with their money in good faith and also that they had a legal right to the buildings because that's what Mr. Simbold had told them. Resolving their moral rights with their legal rights caused them many problems and Sister Maria was not impressed when they started on about karma. It was one thing saying that there had been a fraud somewhere, but unless someone came up with the money that Sister Quiteria and Mr. Simbold had extracted from the Dalai Lama Trust, there seemed no simple solution. The money had mysteriously disappeared from the order's bank account the very day it was paid in.

Of course everyone knew that the signatures of the documents were forgeries, but since Mother Rosalinda had suffered a fatal collapse at her final exhibition, Father Baines, the main witness to the documents, was dead, and Mr. Simbold was not about to incriminate himself by saying anything much at all...reversing the transaction became somewhat complicated. Eventually, Mother Maria was told in no uncertain terms by the Mother House in Italy that given all the bad publicity for the order, it might be an idea to find other premises. They did get some financial compensation eventually via the government who were anxious to keep the whole affair quiet, but it wasn't what the land and property had been worth.

Why Sister Quiteria had wanted to sell the convent as well as getting the money from the sale of the fuel rod apart from funding her "escape" no one was quite sure, but Detective Inspector Vale told Mother Maria that his opinion was that she was "simply evil." He'd said, "It's really not a lot more complicated than that." When pressed further, he added philosophically, "When you're on the run, everything costs."

Of course it was more complicated than that, but for reasons of national security, no one was going to expand much further on how. Nobody ever really discovered why she'd been "on the run" in the first place except those who knew and those who knew parts of the story, but only on a need-to-know basis. *It's sort of comforting in a way to know that D notices do still work a bit even in the 21st century*, thought Mother Maria.

Mr. Simbold avoided prosecution for his part in the sale of the convent and for running over policemen, but his political career never recovered from the stigma of being "the politician who steals from nuns and runs over policemen," even if none of it was actually his fault. He was deselected by his party before the next European Election. Expelled from the United Kingdom Independence Party, he moved on to smaller, more explicitly right wing parties with even smaller memberships and more insane members where his false accounting skills were soon in endless and ever greater demand.

Edmund Salter's relatives were busy taking fairly pointless legal action against the police and the security services for what they describe to websites like CounterPunch and davidicke.com as a "double family state murder" whenever anyone listened. A succession of opposition MPs took on their case from time to time only to lose interest whenever their party got elected to government.

On the plus side, Mr. Salter's widow had become a bit of a celebrity on the conspiracy theories circuit, and there was even talk of a Channel 4 documentary.

Detective Inspector Vale did quite well out of the whole experience, receiving a commendation for bravery. The uranium fuel rod was sent safely to a deep geological repository. Hopefully, it hasn't got lost again.

Mr. Bakir was unceremoniously extradited to a country that didn't feel as though it had to go through the motions of looking as though it observed human rights, much to the delight of the Daily Mail and the Pentagon.

Mother Maria did not have her missio canonica restored, but is now too often on anti-depressants to seriously worry anyone in Rome with her writings.

As to Sister Quiteria, stories vary. Some people held the opinion that she settled in the Philippines...others Brunei. Of course, she could be dead, or maybe in Russia. She was probably somewhere, whoever she was.

About the Author

Anthony E. Miller is a standup comedian and scientist who has performed all over the UK. He is Managing Director of Pear Shaped in Fitzrovia London's 2nd Worst Comedy Club http://www.pearshapedcomedy.com

"possesses a sense of humour so dry it's in danger of being arid." -Doug Devaney, Virtual Brighton Magazine

Go to http://comedycv.co.uk/anthonymiller/index.htm to see more quotes.